Another Man's Love

by

Cheryl A. Cornell

Another Man's Love

Cover Art by *Angela Anderson*

The Wild Rose Press
PO Box 706
Adams Basin, NY 14410-0706
Visit us at www.thewildrosepress.com

Publishing History
First Champagne Rose Edition, 2009
Print ISBN 1-60154-477-4

Published in the United States of America

Dedication

For Rich, my first, second, third, my always.

My thanks to everyone at The Wild Rose Press
for all their support,
especially Roseann Armstrong.

Special thanks to my patient editors,
Lili Booth and Nicole Cherry.

Thanks to Angela Anderson for the cover art.

Another Man's Love

We were never supposed to meet
Fate called our bluff
She's everything I ever wanted
But dared not dream
She's another man's love
She doesn't notice me
She's another man's love
She'll never be free

I have no choice, I walk away
Searching for another way
Her face invades my dreams
She never fades away
She's another man's love
She doesn't notice me
She's another man's love
She'll never be free

Time finds us, but is it too late
No longer his wife, I can't walk away
A second chance to make her mine
Dare I imagine
She's no longer his love
I make her mine
She's now my wife
I'll never set her free

Preface

"You have to be the most obstinate woman I've ever come in contact with!" He let out an exasperated breath and tried to control the anger and fear his voice didn't hide. There was a protracted silence before she finally spoke.

"I can fix that for you," she whispered. "Don't call again, Tom. It's that simple. I'm responsible for myself and to myself. And if you haven't already figured it out, I don't like being second-guessed!"

"Jeez, Corin," he tried, but she cut him off.

"My cell is running low; I need to save the batteries. I'm fine Tom; nothing is going to happen to me."

"I'm not saying you're incapable, I'm just questioning if it's a wise idea to stay there during a major hurricane. If Rand was still alive..." Again his voice had risen and he instantly put himself in check. He could picture her face as clearly as if she stood before him. "I'm sorry, I didn't mean to bring him up, but he told me he had to literally pick you up and carry you to the truck during the last storm. You left for him. Corin, please, do this for me?" It was a dirty, low-down way of going about it, but he was that overwhelmed.

"If Rand were alive we wouldn't be having this conversation." Her statement dared him to dispute her words and he knew better. After another deafening silence she went on. "Tom, I appreciate your concerns, but I'm fine. I really have to go; I have some...details to handle before I lose daylight." It was a stand-off.

1

"Corin, please, just get in the car and drive up here. If you leave now, you could be here in a few hours."

"I can't do that...This is my home, where I belong. If I leave and can't get back, then what?"

He could hear the utter frustration in her voice and knew he was the cause. "And if you stay and have a problem, you're all alone. What if you need help and it can't get to you?" He paced the length of the hotel room once again, trying to figure out how to make her see his point. "Damn it, Corin, it's a house. It can be rebuilt, you can't." He felt the mattress sag under his weight as he sat down heavily.

"You'd be surprised," she mused. "I appreciate the offer but, no thanks. People know I'm here, neighbors and Bob. It will turn out all right, take care Tom," she disconnected the call.

His initial impulse was to call her right back. Instead he let the top half of his body drop back onto the mattress and forced himself to take several long deep breaths. Large fingers rose to rub the sudden ache in his temples then slipped down to rub his closed eyes. Softly at first then harder, pushing his knuckles into the sockets until patterned lights appeared on the inside of his lids. Plaid, he realized and dragged his hands away. The small smirk that followed on his lips made him realize he was in deep, too deep for comfort.

That acknowledgement allowed him to dismiss the cell phone lying on the bed as he walked towards the shower, stripping off his clothes as he went. A quick stop at the mini-bar and a cold green bottle of imported beer helped the ache in his throat. Under the spray of the hot water his mind wandered for the two-hundredth time back to that morning in her kitchen.

Chapter One

He wasn't ever supposed to meet her or them. If bad weather hadn't delayed his initial flight, if he hadn't missed his connection, if his rental car had still been reserved and waiting for him when he finally reached Raleigh, North Carolina. If the man he'd sat across from on the plane hadn't been there taking possession of the last available rental just ahead of him, if he hadn't accepted the ride. But he had. On a cold February evening he'd recognized it was his only way to make it to his destination.

Traveling usually went smoothly for him; years on the road made him a seasoned veteran. He knew better than to travel on Presidents' weekend, but when the call came about the vehicle it seemed like a good way to kill a week off. This trip had gone wrong from the start. Heading in the general direction of his destination, his new companion was congenial and humorous, but talked non-stop most of the way. He also had the keys to the last vehicle that would leave the rental office that day. There were options; he could have booked a room at a nearby hotel and waited until the next day, but he hadn't. He'd accepted the offer of a ride down to Wilmington. He knew better but went against his inner judgment; a decision that changed his life.

Bob Toscano was on his way to visit a cousin who lived just outside the city in the Wrightsville Beach area. He gathered from the conversation it was a favored relative he'd not seen in over a year. The storm worsened through their southeastward trek along the interstate and secondary roads, making a trip of a few hours turn into an almost eight-hour ordeal. The heavy snow they'd left behind in Raleigh turned into an icy sleet mix, then to rain, with what had to be gale-force winds that rocked the small sedan with regularity. He supposed that was why they were both tense when they finally reached the outskirts of the city. Throughout the trip his cell phone had had no reception. Bob had been nice enough to stop at three of the larger hotels for him to grab a room, but none were available. Most people were smart enough to get off the roads during a winter nor'easter.

It wasn't until he'd accepted the stranger's offer to crash at his cousin's house that he allowed his second thought to materialize in his mind. It was too late. They were heading east along country roads in horrendous rain and he wished he'd stayed in Raleigh. Hell, the reality of it was that he wished he'd stayed in Boston.

After what seemed like hours of anxious travel they were now hitting pockets of heavy fog on unlit, narrow back roads with wide ditches on either side. The water could be seen rushing through them each time the lightning struck. Tom Hayden swore to himself he'd never read another horror novel again. The rutted path they turned onto was worse. Narrower and darker, it wasn't until they'd traveled what seemed like a mile they saw the home ahead. The dashboard clock told them it was near midnight. He wasn't sure what to expect but this wasn't it.

The multi-leveled structure seemed to rise from the sand dunes, its weathered cedar siding glinting grey when the headlights flashed on it. Wide porches wrapped the structure on all sides. There were no lights on inside. Only one single fixture shone in the darkness, a beacon to the front door. He heard Bob sigh next to him and refrained from doing the same thing.

"I hope your cousin doesn't mind an extra guest," Tom started. "We probably should have called to let them know."

"Nah, don't worry about it." Bob pulled the vehicle around the circle of plants in the center of the driveway and stopped in front of the main staircase. The home stood on pilings Tom realized, understanding they must be near the beach. "Besides, if I called her about you, than she'd know I was coming."

Turning in his seat, he realized for the first time they would both be unexpected company. "I hope she has a good sense of humor," he mused, realizing he had no other real options at the moment. Past midnight on a horrible, stormy night and he had no available transportation of his own. He decided if things got uncomfortable he would simply call a cab and ask to be taken...he didn't know where to, but he'd worry about that later. Another torrent of rain shook the car and he reluctantly got out.

Bob was leaning on the doorbell and apparently getting no response. As he made his way closer an interior light snapped on, giving the whole place an eerie glow. The wooden inner door opened, and a large, bare-chested man stood defensively in the opening. Deep baying sounds came from a large dog next to him. For several seconds scenes of landing in jail for the night circulated through his mind until recognition swept over the man's face. A low grumbling sound came from beside him a second time, the old tan hound dog defending his territory. "Well I'll be," the burly man started, his southern drawl thicker than Tom expected. "Come in out of the rain, Bobby. Didn't your mama teach you not to stand out in a storm?" With a wide smile and a hearty laugh, lights flicked on temporarily blinding all three men and the beast.

"It's about time you answer the door, Corin had

you tied to the bed again?" Bob teased back, moving aside while the screen door pushed open for their entry. In the large foyer the two men hugged and slapped each other on the back several times before separating. Tom took a tentative step into the marbled space and held back a low whistle, keeping one eye on the questioning dog. The floating mahogany staircase was quite a focal point, not to mention the chandelier that suspended from several floors above. Movement caught his eye and his heart jumped to his throat.

She came from the back of the house, long legs uncovered, and her feet bare. Her toenails were painted a soft pink. Black silk peeked out from under a man's red and black plaid flannel shirt and she was rolling back the sleeves as she neared.

"Rand, is everything all right—Oh, my gawd—" Soft waves of sorrel colored hair covered most of her face until a slim fingered hand raked back the mass of curls. Dark green eyes and soft pouty lips took in the sight in front of her. Tom watched her size up the situation for only a few seconds before letting out a wild scream. With it, she started to run towards them, Bob catching her in his arms as her legs locked around his hips.

The hound started to whine and its owner's hand smoothed his head. Bob and the woman staggered together for a moment then hugged tightly. "I don't believe it," she whispered, "I'm so happy to see you."

From there she let out with a torrent of questions he couldn't keep up with and Bob didn't try. They seemed to have their own short-hand language that he couldn't decipher.

Taking a step forward towards the other man he extended his hand. "I'm Tom Hayden, sorry to have interrupted your evening without any notice," he started. His large hand was swallowed up by the other man's equally massive hand and pumped heartily several times. At that moment the dog seemed to relax; rather he slid to the floor in a mellow motion, landing on his back, his belly exposed.

"Not to worry, we never know when Bob's going to strike..." he said it with humor and Tom saw an honest affection as he watched the other two. She was still locked around Bob's body her hands locked behind his neck, her own head thrown back and she laughed at something he didn't catch. What he finally caught was the sound of her voice, low and throaty with a gravelly touch. She spoke with a northern accent that had been overridden by a southern life. Some words were very Yankee sounding and others were rounded with a southern twang.

"So, who have you brought us this time?" she finally said, recognizing they weren't alone in the foyer. Her legs unwrapped and she slid to the floor before once again dragging the hair from her face with her left hand, the hall light glinting off the row of diamonds on her third finger. Coming forward she extended her right hand to him.

"Welcome to the beach, I'm Corin. Have you met my husband Rand? That walking carpet is Beau, are you afraid of dogs..." She gave him no time to answer; instead she started on a second litany of questions; at that moment a melody dropped into his conscious mind, words swirling with it. "When was the last time you two had anything to eat, how long can you stay, do you have any luggage to bring in before you dry off?"

He lost track and must have seemed startled. "Sorry, you'll get used to us," she said with a laugh, turning back towards Rand. His hand automatically went to her shoulder. "Would you like coffee or tea or something stronger? We have a bottle of burgundy open or, Bob, you know where the bar is, get Tom a drink while I fix us a snack."

All three men were silent for a second and she finally stopped talking, realizing they were staring at her. Tom couldn't help but stare. She was magnificent. Whatever black slip of a thing she was wearing was short on her thighs, the flannel shirt brushing at its hem. The neck of the shirt was open and most of her chest was revealed, along with a large space of cleavage he realized wasn't enhanced by a bra. It was all hers, high and proud and a twinge in his crotch made him look away.

****

The rest of the night was a blur. He was bustled into the kitchen which turned out to be a huge room blended into an informal living and dining area. It had high vaulted ceilings held up by massive beams. There was a roaring fire in the river stone hearth and he realized instantly they'd interrupted a romantic moment for Corin and Rand. She didn't seem affected by the intrusion. With more questions and non-stop tidbits about family she gathered their wine and glasses and brought them to the eating area then grabbed two extras before filling them all. She flipped on the coffeemaker as she went and before he knew it cheese chunks and crackers as well as a huge basket of fruit was being pushed before him on the black granite counter. Corn chips were poured into a cloth napkin lined basket.

Corin was struggling to open a jar of something from the refrigerator. When it didn't budge she moved towards Rand. An automatic movement had him taking the Mason jar from her, twisting it open and handing it back, all the while neither of them lost track of the conversation. She rose up on her toes and left a light kiss on his cheek. The chunky red concoction was poured into a black glass bowl and set before him. Another dish was filled with sugar-coated pecans and slid beside it. Finally a cheesy-looking concoction was dumped into a white bowl.

Tom took one look at it and knew it was pimento cheese spread, his least favorite thing in the world. The whole time none of them mentioned the fact Rand was wearing only old worn jeans and obviously Corin had grabbed his shirt when they were interrupted. Nobody mentioned the obvious fact they'd interrupted their fireside tryst. Each time she reached into an overhead cabinet both items rose along her firm thighs and he had to force himself to look away.

"Okay guys, get started on this and I'll be right back," she said before she disappeared from the kitchen. Rand moved to the fireplace and very nonchalantly tossed the pillows back onto one of the two sofas that flanked it. He settled several large logs on the glowing embers before returning to the kitchen and taking a seat across the counter from him and Bob, their conversation unbroken.

There were no awkward moments between the men, he realized. Whatever the relationship between Bob, Corin and Rand, it was a comfortable one. They teased easily and talked about the weather and the house. When she returned several minutes later he noticed she pulled on a pair of washed-out jeans, soft and thread-bare in spots. Gone was the black silky slip but she still wore the flannel shirt, only now it was buttoned higher towards her throat. Thankfully, she was still barefoot, the tips of her fingernails matching her painted toenails. Her hair had been brushed but not tamed. Tom didn't know why this struck him, he'd never considered himself a foot man before and still didn't, but something about her made him hard just looking at her.

Remembering his place in the situation he forced himself to take in the space around them. It was new, yet looked lived-in. Pots of all shapes and sizes hung from a suspended wrought iron rack over the cook top. The counters held large canisters of all shapes and colors. Some proudly told him what their contents were; others were hiding their secrets. Above the upper cabinets a collection of vintage cookie jars was proudly displayed. From the Pillsbury dough boy to a paint-flecked matched pair of jazz musicians, he'd never seen so many different ones. Some resembled animals or building, others were abstract. There were several tucked among the countertops, too.

Corin brought one forward after reaching for a plate from a nearby cabinet. The grey elephant's head was removed by the trunk as she dug inside, placing oatmeal cookies on the plate. When she came forward with them she gave him a distracted smile before going to the freezer. Something in a square plastic container was put beside the coffee pot before she took a seat beside Rand. His arm automatically went to the back of her stool, his thumb absently rubbing her back. The conversation around him remained on family members and an apparently upcoming wedding.

Tom saw the same coloring and same green eyes, same brown hair and facial expressions. They could have been brother and sister, but cousins fit too.

"I know she's not your favorite cousin," Corin started and was interrupted.

"Of course not, you are," Bob teased back as he layered the cheese spread on a cracker. He ate it in one bite and Tom's stomach rolled.

"That goes without saying, but you could help her."

"Oh please, no matter what anyone does or says she's still likely to look like the proverbial meringue. Let's just plop her on top of the cake and be done with it."

"James might like that, think of the places he'd find frosting..."

"If only James knew what to do when he found it," Bob quipped back and they both laughed. Rand interceded.

"Don't mind these two," he told Tom. "It's a strange family." Tom only nodded then asked about the house. Distracted from the family conversation, he listened to Rand's descriptions of the way Corin had found the house and realized she had masterminded the reconstruction, brought it back to its current state.

"Hell, there was a family of bats living in the fireplace," Rand continued. "Windows were missing, the rain and salt air had swept though the old place for years." He shook his head at a memory he didn't share. "But she had a vision and while it damn near killed us both, it's quite a place now. I can't imagine living anywhere else. In the morning, if the storm passes you'll understand why it was worth the hassle."

All four of them had picked at the snacks laid before them, Tom tentatively tasted the red muck. How could he not when the other three were scooping it up with chips like there was no tomorrow. When he did finally take a taste it surprised him. A homemade concoction similar to a salsa, this one was sweet with a hint of sour behind it. The salt of the chips balanced it out. Quite a taste he decided as he took another chip loaded with it. Rand asked about Tom's reason for being in the area and was surprised to hear anyone would travel from Boston to take delivery of a vehicle.

"I had a few days off and figured the drive back north would be relaxing. That was the initial plan, anyway. Since the weather has played havoc with my flights, I'm going to have to arrange to pick it up tomorrow."

"Good luck with that, if you can get the dealer between church and golf you're a better man than most around here."

"The salesman told me to call him when I reached the area and he'd accommodate me. I'll be out of your hair in the morning."

"No hurry, Sunday suppers around here get...interesting." Rand stood and pressed a kiss to Corin's temple. Her hand reached to his arm as he did but she didn't stop her conversation with Bob.

This was the second time he'd heard mention of Sunday suppers at Corin's house. On the plane he and Bob had talked superficially about their travels and it was Bob's intention to get to his cousin's before the meal. He still wasn't sure what mystery the meal held, but he knew he'd be long gone before it started. It was hard not to stare at her. Her face scrubbed clean, her hair a mass of dark, tangled curls falling around her shoulders and her smile seemed to light up the room.

Rand moved away and gathered mugs. Corin seemed quite content to let him get the coffee things out. Finding he was watching her again he moved from his seat towards the living area, coming to stand before the fire, his hands automatically warming against the heat. The picture above it had caught his eye when they'd entered the space, now he took the time to study it.

The seascape was impressionist, yet had an amazing amount of detail. When he glanced back towards the kitchen Corin and Bob were in a heated discussion that resulted in a huge laugh with Rand's input. Several minutes later the lighting changed behind him, a portrait light illuminated the seascape and he turned to see Rand watching him.

"It's amazing isn't it," he started. "From some angles it's only color and brush strokes, but from others they build into this breathtaking ocean scene."

"I agree I've never seen anything quite like it." He went closer to the painting and studied it in the better light. There were scrawled initials in the bottom corner but he couldn't make them out.

"I doubt you will again. Corin changed her style a few years back, you should see some of the stuff she does now. Much more assured, but there's something about this one...It's almost chaste..." Tom accepted the information he'd been given.

Tom realized his stunned reaction made Rand proud. "Maybe tomorrow, if she's in the mood, she'll show you some of her other works," he added before telling Tom the coffee was ready. Both men headed back towards the counter area but Tom stopped several times taking a second and third look at it from the distance. He shook his head with disbelief when he returned to the group.

Corin was stacking lemon bars on a china plate emblazoned with a yellow and black stripe running across it. He was immediately taken by the taste of the coffee and that discussion launched several others. It was after three when Rand moved back in his seat, stretching his neck from side to side.

Corin's hand reached to massage it for him breaking the moment. Cups and dishes were gathered and quickly stowed in one of the two dishwashers. There was none of the salsa left or the chips. One lonely lemon bar stood waiting for its destiny, the oatmeal cookies having long disappeared. Tom watched Rand take the last bar from the plate before unceremoniously dumping it onto a lower rack. He took one large bite of the tart confection then moved next to his wife at the sink, holding it just a few inches from her mouth. Their forms reflected in the window and gave Tom a clear view. There were several muttered words he couldn't make out before the bite was lowered to her extended tongue. The intimate moment between them stirred something in his belly he'd long forgotten once existed.

****

Thankful to be heading to a bed and away from the distraction of Bob's cousin, Tom found himself eyeing the space around him, his fingers itching to touch the walls he walked amongst. At the top of the stairs Rand told him to turn to the left. He glimpsed a single door to the right, three steps leading to it at the end of a short hallway and knew immediately it was their master bedroom. Again his body reacted. Bob was still going on about something and he wondered if the man ever shut up. Corin's laugh made it all worthwhile.

"The usual?" he asked, and Rand nodded. Bob opened the first door on the right as they entered the corridor. Tom got a glance of a white and tan bedroom. Bold stripes all but jumped from the walls to the hallway. Corin paused beside Bob and Rand motioned for Tom to continue. At the last doorway Rand's hand pushed open the door revealing a blue and white guest room.

"Bathroom's through that door and closet's on the other side. If you need anything just let one of us know. Bob pretty much knows his way around too." The two men paused and stared at each other for a few seconds, seconds too long. Rand said nothing but headed towards the door. "Make yourself comfortable, we're a relaxed household. Corin wouldn't have it any other way. Coffee pot's set up, if you're first up just flip the switch. Feel free to rummage in the kitchen."

"Thanks, but once the sun comes up I'll be out of your way."

"No problem. You're a friend of Bob's, that makes you welcome here."

"I appreciate your hospitality. But I'll be gone early."

"Let me know if you need a ride in the morning."

"Thanks, I will, unless I can get a cab."

Then Corin paused in the doorway. She gave the room an appraising glance and seemed satisfied. Entering the space she went to Rand, her head resting on his shoulder from behind as her hands dropped onto his upper arms.

"Anything you need?" she asked, before launching into another litany of where everything was including toiletries and extra pillows.

"No, this is fine. It's a beautiful room," he added quickly.

"Thanks," she said distractedly. "See you in the morning, Tom."

He nodded and watched the couple disappear from his sight. Only then did he let his weight drop onto the bed. What a night! He didn't bother to unpack, rather took his shaving kit from his bag now propped open on a large wooden chest near the door. The bathroom was larger than he'd figured. There was a white pedestal sink on the back wall, a large window over it. Standing before it he could hear the ocean beyond but couldn't see anything. Instead it was a huge, extremely dark view. A mirror on the wall to the right of him echoed the window view as well as being practical. There was a standard combination tub and shower but there were several shower heads positioned at different levels. He turned on the highest one running his hand under the spray to test the temperature. The toilet was on the far end, separated by a half wall. Across from it was a large chrome rack stacked with fluffy white and navy blue towels. He grabbed one and jumped under the spray, hoping to clear his mind. It made him feel better and instantly cemented the idea in his brain he had to get away from her soon.

He was a man of the world, he'd traveled widely and given his profession he'd lived a varied and sometimes hectic life. He also knew his host was well aware of him watching his wife. There was no need for verbal confirmation; the strained silence when they'd entered the room had been a non-verbal reminder he was in another man's home. He could respect that. Hell, if Corin were his wife he'd probably be loath to let her out of his sight. Yet that wasn't fair. Dried and spread out on the queen size bed, he tucked his hands behind his head and thought over the last hours.

She never acknowledged him as a man or as male, only as a guest her beloved cousin brought along. She was polite and friendly but never gave him a real reason to think her motives were anything but hostess-like. Corin made a point of including him in the conversations but hadn't dwelled on him. He realized it was what made her so much more attractive to him. Most of his adult life women swooned around him. Corin didn't seem to care. They'd touched on his profession only lightly, the subject being dropped when he wasn't very informative.

Instead, he shared a few funny travel horror stories from his years on the road. He'd been accepted but not fawned over. He knew it was stupid to be disappointed by the one thing he always said drove him crazy. Yet from Corin, recognition would have meant something.

Rand was another enigma. He stood comparable to Tom's six foot plus height and was similar in body frame. The difference was Rand's black hair and dark brown eyes countered Tom's blonde hair and hazel eyes. Never was it mentioned what he or Bob did for a living. It was only hinted at that Corin was an artist, but he didn't know for sure if it was her hobby or profession.

The house around him was quite a structure and from the little he'd been told, the end result he now lounged in must have been a long road traveled. He'd done some home renovation and it drove him crazy. He'd never picked up a hammer or paint brush; rather approved sketches and paint swatches and wrote checks. His mind wandered and he was curious what her bedroom looked like. He wondered further if they resumed their lovemaking behind closed doors. Tom groaned aloud and dragged the down quilt over his naked body. The softness of the navy linen against his skin gave him a chill and he found himself drifting towards sleep with an erection that wouldn't subside.

Chapter Two

Sun drenched his pillow and he scrubbed his hand across his face. It seemed like he'd just closed his eyes yet he understood it was morning and he had to get the hell out of here. Checking his watch on the bedside table it was before seven, too early to call his salesman. Awake, he could smell the coffee brewing and knew he wouldn't get back to sleep. Tom pulled on his sweats and grabbed a clean tee shirt from his case before heading to the bath to brush his teeth and drench his tired face with cool water. In the morning light the room was extremely bright, forcing his eyes to half-close against the glare of daylight beaming through the large window and reflecting mirror. His first daylight look at his surroundings, and what a view. The ocean lay at the end of their land, inviting and intense. A strong wind blew the multi-colored wind sock at the end of the pier straight towards the house. Tom didn't know how long he stood there absorbed in the view but the smell of the brewing coffee wafted up to him again.

Downstairs he heard voices and headed towards the kitchen. The coffee pot was spitting out the last of its liquid gold as he entered the room. Empty, he wandered towards the window over the sink and again heard voices, Corin's low laugh returned by Rand's. They were in the pantry, it wasn't until he neared the far counter he caught sight of them. Tom stopped dead in his tracks, quickly reversing from the room. He made his way back upstairs and closed his door before sinking down on the side of the bed.

His head dropped into his hands, he knew he'd never forget the intimate image of them wrapped in each others arms.

Noise from the next room made him try to put the incident out of his mind and he forced himself to venture out into the hallway once more.

Bob was about to head downstairs when he heard Tom behind him, pausing for him to catch up. "Morning, how did you sleep? I smelled the coffee, you too?"

The running monologue continued until they reached the kitchen. There, Rand stood just pouring coffee into a mug, a contented smile on his face. Tom wondered if he realized he wore an orgasmic grin and knew he wouldn't care. Corin was nowhere to be seen.

Acknowledging his guests with a nod, he moved to a cabinet behind him, taking down similar mugs. After filling each and handing them around he finally spoke. "How did you sleep?" Bob's motor mouth was off and running and Tom tried to tune him out while sipping the hearty brew. Corin, it seemed had gone for a run and would be back shortly to start breakfast. They agreed they'd wait for food until then. Rand pulled down a small flat screen from under a cabinet nearby and found world news. All three men watched quietly and listened until the first pot of coffee was drained. Bob made a production of setting up for a second go round when Rand excused himself.

Tom did too; citing a hot shower was just what he needed. A cold one was more like it, he realized, confirming he hadn't had the balls to meet Rand's eyes this morning.

Taking matters into his own hand so to speak while warm water sluiced over him from the three shower heads he couldn't get the image of them from his mind. He'd never thought of himself as a voyeur before and this was slightly creepy from that point of view. On the other hand, he'd simply walked into a common room in their home; it wasn't like he'd walked into their bedroom without knocking. Still, it left an image he knew he'd have to try hard to forget. It wasn't just that they were having sex; it was that they were loving each other with an intensity he'd long forgotten could exist. The connection they shared was a rare quality and it made him think of his music partner, Joe and his wife, Anna. They seemed to have a similar bond, an all consuming love and understanding that left a portion of the world outside their door.

****

Twelve years earlier when Joe and Anna first met, it almost ended their musical partnership. They'd weathered the stormy road and ultimately found a comfort zone. Instead of traveling together as they had done for the ten years before, they each had their own private tour bus. Joe and Anna had their private time and Tom had his. For a while his second wife Amber had traveled with him as Anna did, but they both knew she didn't like it. The inconvenience of touring the states six months of the year bored her. Only at each performance did she come alive. The rest of the time she hated it and wasn't afraid to let anyone and everyone she met know.

When Anna gave birth to twin girls nine years ago it had been the beginning of the end of his second marriage. Amber wanted children and saw Anna raising her family on the road. Tom knew a child couldn't fix their relationship and refused to participate. He'd known the moment he stepped into the doctor's office for his vasectomy that divorce was eminent. Never letting on he'd had the procedure, she left him for a record producer they met in Texas who impregnated her almost immediately. Last he heard she was driving the other man crazy. The realization always left him with an odd grin. She'd gotten exactly what she wanted yet it still wasn't enough. Tom was thankful he hadn't given into her whim of parenthood.

Seeing Corin and Rand together reinforced the lack of closeness he'd had with both of his wives. Than again, he hadn't chosen well. He could picture Corin easily fitting into the road life, making him a home away from home on their bus, using their travel time constructively. Shaking the idea from his mind he forced himself to get moving. The quicker he was away from her, the better off they'd all be.

Dried and dressed, somewhat sated, he tried the salesman and found his cell had died. There wasn't a phone in his room so he knew he'd have to venture downstairs. The kitchen was empty so he helped himself to the cordless unit built into the side of a cabinet. He had just finished leaving a brusque message when she came through the doorway, breathing heavy and sweaty. She dried off her face with a small towel and toed off her sneakers. Dropping gracefully to grab them, she tossed them behind her into a utility area.

"Coffee," she groaned and seemed not to notice him until she had a mug firmly pressed between both her hands and had taken several long sips. Only than did she turn to him and smile. "Morning, did you get some sleep, anything you need, what would you like for breakfast, how's sausage and French toast sound. Maybe I'll make some blueberry muffins, does that sound better?"

Her monologue went on a while longer until she paused to look at him. "What, you don't like sausage or muffins?" The confused look on her face made him burst out laughing. Again she gave him a quizzical look, "What?"

"I don't know which question to answer first, let

alone remember them all," he teased.

"Spend any length of time with her and you'll get to understand her." Bob had come in quietly. Tom wondered what the two of them looked like to the third man.

"I could say the same thing about you," Tom told Bob.

"Yeah, well..."

"I'm going for a quick shower, then I'll start breakfast." Refilling her mug, the discussion turned back to the menu which Bob had a great deal of input. "Fine, you rinse the berries and I'll make pancakes instead."

Gone as quickly as she appeared, he filled his cup and was thankful Rand entered with the Sunday newspaper. The diversion gave him time to watch the situation around him. Corin returned in jeans and sneakers with her damp hair drying around her face in large curls. She was efficient in her cooking techniques, cleaning as she went. First she put sausages into a heavy black cast-iron skillet that must have been generations old. Batter was made from scratch and set aside. Adept fingers quickly made dough then cut it into small biscuits before being popped into a pre-heated oven. When the sausages were draining on paper towel, slices of ham were quickly sautéed. Bob rose and gathered dishes and silverware and after some discussion decided they'd eat at the counter.

Equal amounts of batter were poured onto the heated griddle in the center of the six burner cook top, blueberries being scattered on top as they started to cook. With a second batch cooking, Corin disappeared into the pantry and called out to Rand to join her. Bob reminded them loudly about breakfast and they came back in smiling mysteriously at each other, Rand carrying a mason jar. He opened the jar and poured its contents into a small pot, deferring to Corin about how many cinnamon sticks to add. In an amazingly short time their feast was before them. A huge platter of blueberry pancakes was placed beside a plate of sausages. The biscuits were split and layered with the salty country ham. The hot syrup was strained into a beige ceramic pitcher before they all settled down to eat.

Tom couldn't remember a meal that tasted so good. Was it because Corin had made it or because she was there? None of it mattered. When they finished he tried the salesman again only to get the same recording. He made himself useful by helping to clear the breakfast mess and accepted Rand's offer of an outdoor tour.

****

Rand explained that the two and a half acre plot was situated at the point of a peninsula. They owned nine hundred feet of bullheaded shoreline. There was a spectacular free-form swimming pool with an infinity edge nestled near the house in the center of a tropical garden. The manicured lawn was green even in the February cold. They discussed the type of grass Corin had planted so it would stay green most of the year. He could picture the place in summer. It would be lush and green and flowers would highlight it with color. A large dock at the end of the pier anchored the extension over a hundred feet into the deep water. They discussed the plastic "wood look" product used for its construction as opposed to regular lumber or pressure treated wood. He began to think about the location. Rand went on to tell him about the storms and how the last pier had been destroyed by Hurricane Ernesto years before.

"God, what a storm, we'd only just finished the pier and the dock. You have no idea what it took to get Corin to leave. Not that I wanted to go, but I

23

knew if we stayed I couldn't guarantee her safety. I literally had to pick her up, toss her over my shoulder and carry her out to the truck to get her away."

"What happened?" Tom prompted.

"The storm took the dock and the pier and most of the landscaping. The pool wasn't in at that point, and Corin had drawings of the garden but she hadn't planted it yet."

"And the house?" Somehow he wanted to know, needed to know. From this perspective it looked strong enough to weather any storm. It was an odd feeling he got, one of instant protectiveness for the structure and its owners.

"Some minor wind damage, roof shingles, some siding needed to be replaced. But the old girl held strong. Of course, Corin wouldn't have had it any other way. It was like the house knew how much she loved it and appreciated being taken care of again."

"Again?"

"It was empty for eight years, caught up in an estate situation. None of them wanted to give it up but none of them did anything to maintain it. By the time Corin found it...well, she managed to talk them into selling it to her. I still don't know what she actually said to them, rather I think she appealed to them on a base level, she saw it as a home that needed tending and living in, they saw it as a commodity. She simply bought their commodity."

"Were you able to move right away or...?"

Rand's laugh cut off his words. "No. We lived in the small apartment over the garage." He nodded towards the far side of the property. All Tom could see was the back of a structure, one he'd missed on his way in last night. Now in the daylight from this angle, he realized there was a large expanse of glass on either end of the upper floor. "It took us two years to bring her up to code before we could get a certificate of occupancy, another year of redoing the interiors."

"You did an amazing job of the renovation."

"Corin did. I just nodded and let her vent when orders were late or the builder couldn't see her vision."

Corin wandered towards them, a heavy shawl wrapped around her shoulders, the old hound walking beside her. Automatically she reached a hand to Rand and was swallowed up against his body.

"I've come to bring news. Your salesman called, he's tied up with a family thing until two, and he'll call you then to set something up."

"Oh, thanks. I suppose I should get a cab into town and..."

"And what?" she asked with a laugh. "No, it's better to just relax and wait until he calls. He said he'd try and deliver the truck to you here to save you the trip."

"Oh."

"Looks like you'll get to sample Sunday supper after all."

"I don't want to intrude," he started but was stopped dead.

"You're not intruding. In fact, by tonight, you may want to run screaming into the night to get away from all of us."

"All of you?"

"Yeah, third Sunday of the month," Rand supplied.

"I've got bread dough to see to, catch you guys later." She reached up for a quick press of her lips against Rand's and moved smoothly away, the animal dogging her steps.

"What am I missing about supper?"

"When we first moved in, people had a way of dropping by on Sunday afternoons to see the project.

After a while it seemed like every weekend we were throwing impromptu parties. When the house was ready to move into, we let everyone gently know our weekends were now off limits, except for the third Sunday. Then it was open house and all were welcome. It's worked out into a nice routine. Corin likes having company to fuss over occasionally and I have the rest of the month to forget about them and gear up for them again."

He was joking but there was an undercurrent of strong truth to his words. This was a couple who learned to accommodate each other, adjusting their habits to make the other comfortable. In a flash he remembered his two marriages. Neither of his wives would be so accommodating.

****

Back inside it looked like she was going to feed the masses. Bob was working on one side of the counter, chopping vegetables in tune to the oldies station on the radio. Corin was almost elbow deep in some kind of rich dough, her hips swaying with rhythm as her hands kept beat in the floury mass. The cooktop held several huge pots all simmering something different. Something was baking in the oven, the smell enveloping the space.

"Can I help or should I stay out of the way?" Tom asked.

"You're on vacation, you should relax. Rand's probably on the front porch with the rest of the paper. Why not join him for an hour or two? I'll let you both know when I need help."

Sweetly dismissed he stepped over Beau, wandering to the front porch and found Rand exactly as she predicted. Blocked from the wind, he sat in a wooden Adirondack chair, the paper open in his lap. His head rested against the back, his eyes shut. Tom took a second chair and extra section of the paper. Before long, he felt his eyelids getting heavy and gave into closing them for just a minute.

****

It was an amazing sight to open his eyes and find a new version of Corin standing over him. The top and sides of her hair were tamed back from her face but several long tendrils on each side refused to be subdued. She wore pink gloss on her lips and had darkened her lashes. Her smile was wide and warm. Not welcoming, the way she looked at her husband, but friendly.

"Sorry, I guess I dropped off there." He glanced around and Rand was nowhere to be found. Stretching his arms above his head, she grabbed at the section of newspaper he'd forgotten was on his lap, the slight brush of her fingers against his knee giving him an instant erection. She sat across from him folding the paper.

"Rand went for a run. He'll be back before company gets here." For the first time he watched her hesitate. She allowed herself one long lingering look before letting her lips fade into a soft smile. "I am the bearer of unfortunate news," she started. Tom was thankful she spoke; he was just about to reach across to her and pull her down to meet his lips. "Your truck has developed a mechanical problem, something with the electrical system. They're towing it back to the shop and will call later when they know what the problem is."

"Oh," he managed to strangle out. He'd completely forgotten about the damn thing. Wasn't that his reason for being here? "I suppose I should get a cab into town and meet them at the shop then, see what's happening."

"It's one alternative, the other is to hang with us and wait until they call back. Are you a mechanic at heart?" she teased, laughing when he reluctantly shook his head no.

"Well, unless you're uncomfortable with us, why

not let them do their job?"

"I've imposed on your hospitality already..."

"Nonsense, it's the third Sunday of the month. All are welcome."

"What would have happened if Bob turned up next week or last week?" His voice teased her with the question but they both knew he really wanted an honest answer.

"We accept Bob whenever he shows up. Usually he picks the third weekend so he can see some other friends and it gives him a chance to play in the kitchen."

She hesitated before adding, "We don't get a lot of company the rest of the month but we do have an active social life. Rand just likes to enjoy it away from here."

"He's very protective of you and your home."

"Yes, he is and so am I. I don't apologize for that. We've come a long way together, Rand and I, and the house. If you think he's protective, then I'm obsessed." Her tone was still soft but he understood. Don't mess with her man or her home.

Tom studied her in the afternoon light. He liked her, plain and simple. Besides being sexually attracted to her, she was a nice woman, who didn't apologize for loving her man or her home.

Tom spoke before he could stop himself. "Neither of my wives cared about our homes, only the addresses."

There was a long pause before she answered him, searching his face. "I'm sorry..."

Corin studied the man on her porch. His blonde hair was natural, his hazel eyes glinted green in certain lights. She figured him to be around Rand's age, mid-forties and well maintained. He stood over six foot and his hands intrigued her.

For Corin, it was always a man's hands that swayed her. Prissy hands wouldn't touch her in any way. Rand's fingers were slightly calloused yet tender when they touched her. His fingers were long and thick, just like the rest of his anatomy. But more importantly, she understood some men knew how to touch a woman. They were usually the creative ones, men who worked with them daily and knew the power they held. Corin knew Tom was a musician, knew his fingers would play a woman's body with the same grace and intensity he used with a guitar or a piano. And she knew without a doubt if he wanted to, he could play her body into submission.

The thought of them together struck her hard. Not once, since she'd met Rand had she entertained the thought of another man. While she'd never seriously do anything to jeopardize her relationship, Tom Hayden made her mind work in an uncomfortable direction. Probably just idol worship in its purest form; there was a copy of all of Hayden and Haas albums in their collection. While mostly popular for their early metal rock songs, their matured works had diversified into blues and even a little country.

And now here he was, a rock-n-roll icon sitting on her front porch. Life was strange she decided but didn't share the thought with him. Instead she cleared her throat and knew to change the subject. She realized he was watching her and she felt her cheeks flush hot. Her hands moved to the dog's head that dropped on her leg, her fingers rubbing the dog's eyes. Corin saw Tom smile and realized he was watching her half amazed as the hound pushed his head towards her hands.

"That's enough, Beau; you're probably seeing plaid by now." Her words were said with a laugh as she gently moved the dog from her lap.

"You give your dog eye rubs," he said aloud.

"Occasionally, it feels good once in a while, doesn't it?" While her statement made sense he'd never thought about it before. He decided she was an odd woman at times and tried to change the subject.

"If you're sure I won't be in the way?" Tom ventured.

"I'm sure, no worries, Tom. But there is one thing we need to discuss." She stood to put the newspaper section on the chair across from him. She grew serious and measured her words. "Last night we glossed over who you are and what you do for a living. I'm not sure some of our guests won't want more than that from you. I need to know how you'd like to handle the situation."

He groaned, accepting her statement. She was right, someone would probably catch on. He spoke freely, her smile comforting. "In all honesty, since I've been here with you...and Rand, I almost forgot who I was." There was a tense silence between them.

"Thank you Tom, that's an extremely generous compliment."

"It's the truth, Corin." She blushed hot a second time.

"But some of our friends..."

"Let's just introduce me as Bob's friend from Boston. If they press further it doesn't pay to lie. I'll simply say my throat is sore and I'm supposed to be resting it. That usually stops any requests for an impromptu performance."

"All right, that sounds workable. But, if anyone gets under your skin, just let one of us know and we'll come bail you out."

"Thanks, but don't worry about me. You should be enjoying your company."

"Oh, I will, for the first few hours, than I'll be wishing the clock to fast forward to get them out of my space." She laughed at his quizzical reaction. "I love my friends, but in small doses." Thinking before she spoke she seemed to steady her words.

"We, Rand and I, enjoy company. But when we

first started working on the old place it seemed every weekend we were entertaining. It got old after a while. That's when we came up with the third Sunday open house. We all get what we want from it. I get to cook and see friends but in a controlled atmosphere."

"I see."

"Do you?" she found herself challenging.

"To a point, is it Rand that doesn't like people around all the time?"

"Yes, but me too, I like company when I'm in the mood. The rest of the time I want the world to disappear and leave me alone here with Rand and our work."

"Why?"

"As Rand would say, in general, 'people suck'. The more you let them influence your daily life the less privacy you retain."

"Okay, I can grasp that concept, to a point."

"Look at it this way, when you're in the mood to write your songs, wouldn't you rather be left alone to do just that. Don't people in general annoy you when they interrupt the process? And after the interruptions, can you ever get back to that same place? I mean, the general idea is still present, but sometimes don't you lose a layer?"

"Jeez, Corin, yeah, I guess so. I'm used to going into the studio and not coming out until I'm ready."

"It's the same for us. If I'm in the studio and get interrupted I generally don't get that flow back. Sometimes the rest of my day is shot. It's the same with Rand. When he goes into his office and shuts the door, he wants the world to stay out of his creative process."

"What do you do?" he asked, leaning forward.

"I paint some and Rand writes."

"The painting over the fireplace, I've never seen anything quite so beautiful in an abstract way. Your style is interesting."

"Thanks, I've always had a fondness for that piece; it was the first one I did after we found the house...it just seems to fit there."

"Do you sell your work in any local galleries?"

"Some pieces, others never get seen and a few make their way to a small shop in New York City."

"That's it," he exclaimed, clapping his hands together. "Soho, right?" She smiled and gave him a short nod. "God that was years ago, probably nine or ten. We were touring with the Silent Applause album. I've seen some of your other work. You do amazing things with color, Corin." He hesitated briefly before adding, "But they were different, more somber and controlled, almost melancholy compared to the one over the fireplace."

"Yes," she acknowledged before finishing with, "those were done after the accident. I was in a different state of mind, despondent and angry." Something about the tone of her voice asked him not to push for more information.

"I'd love to see what you're currently working on, or any of your works. Were you always an artist?"

"Only as a hobby, really, I used to work with a restoration group. We'd travel to different museums and private collections defining the best ways to clean and preserve different works."

"That must have been interesting work."

"It was, for a while. I got to see so many amazing paintings, all over the world. It was very humbling work actually, knowing the masterpiece you touched was irreplaceable was nerve-wracking sometimes, mostly awe-inspiring. To realize you were responsible for a work of art that was hundreds of years old, that if I made a mistake...It sometimes made me anxious to think about what I did."

"And you don't do that anymore?"

"No, not for a while now. I didn't want to be away from Rand and once we moved down here I...lost track of contacts. Occasionally someone will still call. Usually I refer them."

Corin watched Tom realizing he probably figured she turned her back on them for her husband. "Do you miss it?"

"No, I did the job for a while, but that was my old life. Now, with Rand, this is our life together. Just being able to indulge my hobby has been a gift in itself."

"I'd say all your work is a gift."

"It's just how I see the world now," she told him.

"I'd like to see it through your eyes some day, just for a short time. You have a vision that's filled with energy, very spiritual on some levels."

"Thank you. If you're interested there's a few pieces I'm getting ready to ship out, you're welcome to take a look later."

"I'd like that," he said and meant it.

Corin didn't try to over think it. "Well, I should get back to the kitchen; I left Bob icing a spice cake. If I don't get there soon we may have a naked cake and Bob a belly full of cream cheese frosting." She stood and so did he. "Are you hungry or thirsty? Bob just opened a bottle of white wine or we have soda or lemonade. And of course there's always coffee."

They wandered back into the old house side by side and instantly Tom was sorry. He couldn't help but notice how the black leather pants she wore molded to her thighs with each move. Her matching boots lengthened the look, the thin stiletto heels emphasizing her movements. The light green knitted sweater she wore pulled against her bust, the cashmere no match for her God-given attributes. His fingers itched to find their way to her waist to tug her gently against him. He didn't, he followed her back to the kitchen and the bantering of cousins.

He saw the old house around him with a new respect. Corin had seen it as an old master that needed to be restored and she'd done it to the best of her ability. It didn't surprise him now, knowing she'd been into restoration that she'd seen the house as a masterpiece. He appreciated the structure even more now, understanding her need to preserve it.

Chapter Three

A sweaty Rand passed through the kitchen, detouring only to brush his lips across Corin's forehead. They exchanged whispered words and he disappeared as quickly as he appeared. Bob moved beside Tom and nudged him in the ribs. "They're quite a couple, aren't they?"

"Yes, they're both very interesting people. I don't think I remembered to thank you for inviting me."

"Hey, it's the third Sunday..."

"Well, I appreciate it. I'd be stuck in a hotel in Raleigh without your offer."

"I'm sure you see enough of them," Bob added, before heading to the cooktop to stir one of the large pots.

The aroma wafted through the kitchen and struck his empty stomach. It rumbled loudly and Bob laughed at him. His movements around his cousin's kitchen were natural; his cooking talents apparent as he pulled a large roasting pan from one of the wall ovens, checking its contents. The hickory smell enveloped him and he wandered towards it. Bob sliced one of the beef ribs from the end and handed it to Tom. His first bite was heaven, the taste sweet and smoky, the meat all but falling off the bone. He devoured the morsel in record time. Licking his fingers clean he moved to the prep sink to wash them before giving his approval. This time Bob blushed and Tom wondered what he'd gotten himself into.

There was no longer any time to think. The doorbell rang and from then on organized chaos reigned. The dining room he'd passed several times was lit with candles and all the food spread out. It seemed to Tom each person who walked through the door carried some delectable treat. The only morsel Tom wanted to taste was Corin. It had been a long time since he coveted anything; another man's wife was dangerous territory. Glancing at his watch he waited for the phone to ring telling him his vehicle was ready.

Lost in a deep philosophical conversation with Rand and a few of the locals about the ecological systems they relied on, he never heard the phone ring. Corin had passed through the crowded living room, extending the cordless towards him, as she dropped onto the arm of Rand's chair. Her arm around his shoulders, his hand dropped onto her leg, an easy movement, something they'd done hundreds of time he realized. Forcing himself to listen to the conversation at hand, he had to excuse himself to be heard. On the front porch he hit disconnect and cursed aloud.

"There's no problem staying with us tonight, Tom, unless you're uncomfortable?"

He'd felt her presence before he saw her."How could anyone be uncomfortable in your home, Corin? You've made me welcome from the moment I dragged water into your foyer. I've never met a better hostess."

"Then why the pout?" she teased.

"Because..."

"Tom?" He studied her standing just inside the doorway, the wood bracketing her body. It was a look that didn't need words to elaborate. She turned from him and took a breath before speaking.

"If I've given you the wrong idea, Tom I'm sorry. I love Rand and wouldn't do anything ever to jeopardize our relationship."

"*No*, you haven't, Corin. It's just my mind seeing

something that I never had, never dared to imagine I could have." She relaxed back against the door frame and studied him again. He didn't stop to censure his words. "I've never been lucky enough to be loved by a woman the way you love Rand. It's hard for me to accept there really are couples like you. You're so in sync with each other. I see you truly do love him with all your heart. I'd never ask you to risk that. It's too rare."

"Then as long as we understand each other, I don't see any reason for you not to stay. The truck will be fixed tomorrow, why not just relax and hang out?"

"I'd like that."

"Good, I've got to get back inside. When I left, Bob and one of our local fisherman were about to go several rounds about our current president and his policies." She rolled her eyes and they both laughed.

"Just what does cousin Bob do, anyway?"

"Oh, I'd say he's a jack of all trades," Corin told him. "He works with computer programs. I've asked and don't understand any of it. It's easier not to know sometimes." Her face asked him not to question her pat answer further and he didn't. Somehow he now saw Bob as some government personnel and was probably better off not knowing.

Inside, Corin stopped to talk with an older woman in a grey suit. They laughed together then quieted when Bob went on to make a point about foreign policy and funding.

****

As quickly as the chaos started, it came to an end. Sundown came and everyone filtered away with an empty dish. When it was finally down to a core group of about ten, he wandered back into the kitchen. Bob was setting up the coffee maker yet again and asked Tom to grab the spare box of coffee filters from the pantry. Without a second thought he wandered into the dark space, only to find Rand and Corin locked in an embrace. He backed out without the filters. Bob was still talking about something and stopped when he saw Tom's empty hand.

"Oh please, are they at it again? I wish they'd find a room..." He flipped on the overhead light without a second thought and lovingly berated his hosts for holing up in the closet to neck.

"Go away, Bob. You're just jealous." Rand told him, and neither he nor Corin left the space for long moments.

By eight o'clock, night had arrived and Tom found himself staring at the ocean from the rear windows. Actually, he decided, more a wall of glass than windows. The stars lit the sky and the moon glinted off the waves; he felt more peaceful than ever in his life. The irony didn't escape him that his own home had a similar glass wall overlooking the ocean, though he rarely took the time to study his own view.

It seemed quite natural for them to be sitting around the kitchen counter after ten that night. Corin had warmed up leftovers from lunch and they'd all stuffed themselves a second time. Tom never let on that at home he never ate leftovers. It was a pride thing with him. Growing up his family had to watch every penny and that led to lots of creative cooking as his mother used to say. She could take a simple cut of meat and feed her family for two nights and still have leftovers for their lunch. As soon as he started making real money he made himself a promise.

Now, years later, it seemed childish even to him. The lasagna had tasted better the second time and even the minestrone soup that Bob contributed had a melded flavor. He refrained from shaking his head at all the waste he'd created over the years. If either of his ex-wives saw this they'd take him to task. He didn't care. Later they sampled the left-over desserts with another pot of coffee.

Pushing his bar stool from the counter he let out a sigh then a laugh. "No more," he pleaded and Rand just laughed.

"Corin likes to make sure everyone is fed well," he said, teasing his wife as she gave him a cynical look. "If she didn't feed me like this, I wouldn't have to run every day."

"I'm just trying to keep you fit, love. Besides, running does keep your behind in wonderful shape."

"Yeah, that's why you abuse his body at every chance?" Bob asked.

"I'm just trying to keep him heart healthy!"

"Is that what you two call it now," Bob continued, "I'd of thought it as death by sex!"

"You're just jealous," both Rand and Corin said at the same time with a hearty laugh.

"Of course I am," he answered freely. "But because it's you two I'll overlook it."

"Thank you, Bob. I always appreciate it when you allow me to service my wife."

"Oh, please, yuck." Bob let a chill run through him with exaggerated ease.

"Sorry darling, but you've known for years you just don't have the right equipment."

"I know, dear. Just remember that Rand's equipment is for my use."

"Yeah, yeah, but I can dream can't I?" he quipped back.

"Not in my presence or my home," Rand added.

Tom listened to the exchange and wondered about their relationship. Obviously it was a running joke with them, something that bonded them from previous years. Seeing Tom's confused frown, Bob went on.

"You see, I saw Rand first. Only he didn't want any part of little old me. Then I made the mistake of introducing him to Corin and..."

"And he liked my standard equipment much better!" Everyone laughed and Tom fished for information.

"So is that how you two got together, Bob introduced you?" It seemed a harmless question.

"Yes, eventually." Corin hesitated and Rand finished for her.

"When we first met, Corin was married to her first husband. It wasn't until three years later we ran into each other again." He gave her a private smile and reached an arm towards her. She responded by moving from the sink and taking his hand before leaning against his stool. "And I do mean that literally."

Tom gave them a quizzical look.

"We were both out in the Hamptons one weekend and Corin literally backed her Volvo into my new Jaguar. Broadsided my vehicle in a heartbeat. You're a car man, you can relate. They never were able to match the silver metallic paint to the right shade."

"You sold it, didn't you? After the accident, you dumped the car?"

"Absolutely, see, it was his first impulse too."

"So you're both telling me it's a dick thing. Once there's a scratch or minor problem or imperfection with the vehicle it becomes tarnished?"

"Something like that, but only some vehicles," Tom supplied.

"This truck I'm supposed to pick up, I came all the way down here to take delivery because I wanted to make sure it was perfect. Now, after the electrical problems, I'm not sure I'll keep it."

"Keep it; you haven't even bought it yet!" Bob said with a laugh.

"Yeah, but already it's flashing lemon to me. I'm seriously considering walking away from it."

40

"What was it about this particular vehicle?"

"It's a hard color to get, jet black. Fully equipped, man, that baby should be a sight, but now," he mused, letting his face convey the rest of his thought.

"Now there's an imperfection and it's got your stomach in knots?"

"Something like that. I buy new vehicles so I don't have problems on the open road. This one already has problems and I haven't even seen it yet."

"I can understand your feelings, is it going to be reliable when you need it most?"

"Basically, it's a lot of money to spend on a vehicle that might leave me stranded."

"Talk about stranded, Corin almost left me in that parking lot with a trashed Jaguar." He tightened his hold on her and gave her a pleasing smile.

"If you hadn't kept screaming at me, I mean, for God's sake, its metal, glass and leather. It's not like I ran over your dog or your foot." When she said the word "dog," old Beau picked up his head. When he got no attention he dropped it back on his paws.

"No, but it was precious in its own right at the time." Rand sighed. "But then I realized what was truly important in life, and yes, you were right, my love. It was just a hunk of metal and glass. You are worth any number of Jaguars."

"Thank you. I'm glad we got that established." She used her thumb and index finger to mush his lips together before dropping hers on top, leaving him with a wet kiss.

"But you still were at fault, you backed into him..." Bob circled around the conversation leading them back to the beginning.

"Yes, I did, but he was speeding through the lanes like the police were after him, I never stood a chance to stop in time." Rand's arm went around her waist and tugged her onto his lap.

"What he hasn't told you was the fury he started hollering at me with, which set off Beau who decided to protect me from this raving man..." They both laughed again before she continued. "After I promised not to let Beau out of the car we both started to calm down. He was so angry it took him a while to realize who I was, that we'd met through Bob. When he finally stopped screaming long enough to recognize me...Let's just say we didn't need to bring the police into it."

"It's only fair to mention you'd changed your hair completely."

"Yes, I had a different hairstyle from when we first met."

"And you've been together ever since?"

"Only in my dreams. She made me wait and work for her. Almost a whole year before she'd agree to have supper with me."

"Yes, but I was worth the wait," she added as Bob made gagging noises.

"Enough of this fantasy love story. Corin, are you going to make another pot of coffee or does your guest have to do it himself?"

"I don't consider you a guest; you know where the supplies are, get off your butt and fix it."

"Oh, so temperamental, I just love to rile her up." He stood and moved easily through the kitchen setting up the fresh coffee.

"I don't know how any of you sleep around here. I used to think I was a coffee addict, but you three make me look like I'm in the minor leagues."

"That's because it's decaffeinated."

"All of it? All the coffee I've drunk here is decaf? I'd never have believed it."

"Corin's got to be careful with caffeine," Rand replied.

"I get enough with my daily chocolate intake, in

our coffee too, we'd be wired."

"So, you're a chocoholic?"

"Isn't everyone?"

Tom realized he'd seen large bowls of mini chocolate bars in every room. Three distinct kinds graced each container. He'd assumed it was for the open house and couldn't imagine anyone eating that much chocolate.

Chapter Four

That night he fell asleep quickly and slept soundly. He awoke the next morning only to check his watch and see it was after ten. He was back on his personal schedule. But he had obligations and he was a guest in Corin's home; he thought of too many other reasons not to stay in bed, the first one being that he'd see her again. Last night he rationalized with himself he was just infatuated with her, and if they really spent time together, he'd find her flaws and she'd become human to him, just like all the rest of the women he knew. No sensual scent of coffee wafted up the stairs and he figured he was the last one up. Only slightly embarrassed he showered and dressed quickly. Downstairs, the kitchen looked like it did the night before. He flipped on the pot and leaned against the kitchen sink staring out at the ocean while it perked. Tom wasn't sure how long she stood in the doorway behind him before making her presence known.

"Morning," she mumbled as she went through the motions of pulling down mugs and getting the milk from the refrigerator. She moved to the coffee pot using the counter in front of it to hold her up. Her arms heavy at her side dropped to the surface and it was a short drop to let her head lean on them, her eyes closing automatically.

Tom watched the morning ritual with a smile. Had she done the same thing yesterday only Rand was the first one up to meet her? Hunched down as she was her back was pushed out, her bottom all but asking to be fondled. His erection twitched once again. Tom still couldn't remember the last time he'd been affected by a woman this way. He saw too many of them in his work, yet Corin was different. Maybe it was a chemical reaction or lust in its purest form he wondered, thankful the last drops filtered down. Her head popped up and her slim hand reached to fill two mugs. Both of them were in her hands as she brought him one, hers already to her lips.

"Thanks," Tom said. He was just grateful she wasn't spread over the counter in a 'take me quick' position. Somehow he knew he'd never think of silk pajamas the same way.

The phone interrupted them and after some discussion, Tom agreed to see the vehicle before making a final decision. Later that morning after Corin's version of a quick breakfast of bacon and eggs, they all drove into the city. Sales, at the dealership, were happening all around them in honor of the holiday and it was quite congested. He caught sight of Rand checking out one of the latest models but Corin was nowhere to be found. Bob kept trying to make a new friend of one of the salesmen.

Outside with the keys in hand, he went about surveying the vehicle. It was huge, monstrous almost. It was jet black and seemed to be in mint condition. The service manager met him beside it and explained the problem. Finally satisfied, he decided to take delivery of it. Their plan had been to meet for a late lunch at a restaurant just up the road. Bob took the co-pilot seat and seemed impressed by the ride of the military style truck.

"Bob, can I ask you something, something that's none of my business?"

"That depends, is it about us?" Tom gave him a half frowned look and a raised eyebrow. "All right, but a man can dream. What do you want to know about Corin?"

"Between us, she mentioned an accident yesterday but didn't elaborate." For the first time he watched Bob become uncomfortable. He squirmed in the seat and turned to look out the window.

"It's not my place to give you details if she didn't. How did she bring it up?"

"We were talking about some of her earlier paintings, ones I'd seen in a gallery years ago. She said they were her post-accident work."

"Yeah, I have a sketch from that time. She was still working with the museum, actually on medical leave. Nobody was more surprised when the gallery owner asked her for a few pieces to fill in a show. She'd been quite secretive about them until the first showing. They'd known each other from college and the owner loved the darkness in those pieces. Her style has changed but she still sends up a few pieces now and then."

"And?" Tom prompted, getting anxious for details before they reached the restaurant.

"And it was a car accident, her mother was driving and lost control."

"How badly were they hurt?" He stopped for the yellow light delaying their progress. He knew a morbid fascination made him want more details.

"Her mother didn't survive and Corin was critically injured. For the first two weeks we didn't know if she'd make it." Bob turned towards the window again when his eyes became lidded. Tom watched him take measured breaths.

"Jeez," was all Tom managed to hiss out.

"There's a lot more, Tom. But it's Corin's history, not mine. She made an amazing recovery all considered. Please don't bring it up unless she offers. It's getting near April; the first weeks of the month are always difficult."

"No problem, I won't mention it."

"Good. Because if you were involved with her it

might be different, but since you're not..."

"It's none of my business."

"Yeah."

"Okay. So where's this restaurant we're supposed to meet them?"

"Take a left at the next light, it's on the corner."

They spent the rest of the drive discussing the new vehicle which at the moment seemed to be working fine.

Over lunch he was persuaded to spend the night and leave early the next morning. With holiday traffic and the late hour, how far could he get? It seemed logical and he didn't want to leave. When Rand offered up that Corin would make homemade pizza for their supper, he was sold.

****

After midnight he finally gave up and pulled on sweats. The house was quiet around him as he snuck down stairs to the kitchen. He knew there were a few slices of pizza left and the idea made his mouth water. Tom realized one of the most irritating parts of being on the road; there was never a stocked refrigerator when you wanted one at two in the morning. Mini-bars were all right, but they were boring. Sometimes real food, like a sandwich or bowl of cereal would have been his pleasure instead of a cookie or chocolate bar.

Cold pizza slice in hand with a length of paper towel, he wandered the dark, empty rooms of Corin and Rand's home. This was the first opportunity he'd had to stick his head in the front parlor and turned on the first light switch his hand hit. It was a formal room, done in off-white silks and fabrics. She'd mixed silver and gold to complement and it worked. While it was formal, it didn't seem stuffy. It was completely different from the feel of the family room he'd spent so much time in, but still, a pleasant place. The polished black baby grand called to him from the corner. His fingers itched to play it, to hear the tone. He didn't. Instead, he looked at the framed photos on the back.

While he could only assume, he figured out there were pictures of both sets of their parents as well as several candids of themselves. One formal wedding portrait and two group scenes with Bob prominently beside Corin. The wedding one held his gaze. Rand looked much younger, no grey at the temples. Corin looked beautiful with her eyes clear and her dark hair piled on top of her head. While in a semi-traditional gown, it was a soft ivory color, the tailored sheath a foil for her long, lean body. The draped neck hinted at her figure but was deceivingly modest. The rest of it was completely unadorned. Only the wild flowers she held broke the line. Rand stood beside her in a black tuxedo, his tie and shirt a light tan to complement her gown. They looked happy, younger and in love. Her smile reflected a confident woman who knew her choices were right. Tom knew in that very moment he had to get away from her. And more importantly, he should never see her again. For his sanity, he knew to keep away.

****

Another man's love, another man's wife. Never before had he become infatuated with another man's woman. After this afternoon he knew he was falling hard and the experience was totally unwarranted. While wandering around her studio, Tom had seen some nude sketches of a well-appointed man. He didn't need to ask, he knew they were of Rand even though the facial features weren't roughed in. He tried to avoid them but her style had his eyes scanning back towards them. He tried to focus on the female nudes and moved away when he realized they were self portraits. Bob was on his cell phone in the living room area, his call about business. Corin moved beside him and smiled before laughing openly.

"It was one way to break the ice..."

"Excuse me?" Tom said, not sure where she was going with her words. "The nudes, it was one way of checking out Rand's equipment..." She paused before laughing openly at his discomfort. "I've embarrassed you, Tom. I'm sorry."

"No...Yes, I'm confused," he relented.

"When Rand and I had been dating for a while I was still apprehensive about starting a sexual relationship with him, hell, with any man. After my divorce it was easier to retreat. I was still scarred, physically and emotionally. But I knew he'd be different."

"Was it a dare, asking him to pose for you?"

"I suppose you could look at it from that perspective. In actuality, I'd wanted to sketch him from the first time we met. There was something about him, something I was drawn to on a core level."

"And after you got his clothes off?"

Corin blushed but didn't retreat.

"I had to know if he had depth before our relationship went any further."

"I don't understand."

"That's because you're a man." She laughed and he watched as she chose her words carefully. "I was young when I met my first husband. Our relationship was good but immature. When Rand came into my life I knew I wanted more from him. I had to know if he could make me...fly."

"Fly?" Tom was confused, more so than he liked or wanted to acknowledge. Again Corin's lips lifted into a smile.

"In a manner of speaking, I had to know if he could be my safe place."

"As in..."

"Sex of course, I thought that was what we were

talking about."

"Just making sure I hadn't taken a wrong turn." He studied the upper torso sketches on the back wall, opting not to stare at Corin's version of her husband's equipment.

"I can only assume he set you free?"

She laughed and the sound of her voice hit him to the core level, his erection growing.

"I knew I couldn't be in a relationship with a man who didn't understand my body."

"Apparently you two came to terms..."

"Eventually, once I realized he understood and truly appreciated what we could share. It's not just about the actual act, so much as the mind set that gets you there."

"Safe haven?" Tom asked, trying to associate her thoughts in his mind.

"Close. Haven't you ever wanted to just let loose, to be able to go primal and know your partner won't hold it against you in the morning?"

"Isn't that what marriage is supposed to be about?"

"I believe so, but it wasn't like that when I was married to Ted. Maybe because we were young, both inexperienced. But when I met Rand, besides being attracted to his body and his mind, I knew he'd understand sometimes between partners there are moments of...primitive free fall. A place you work towards where you're completely free to let go and just experience. It's a liberating encounter, to find a person you trust to truly be yourself with...no holding back. And most of all, knowing it won't get used against you in a moment of anger or disdain at a later date."

"He must be really good," Tom whispered, blushing when she smiled at him.

"Yes, he's a wonderful lover and partner. But just because he uses his equipment with skill doesn't mean the trust is automatically there. To truly find that place where nothing you do together is considered immoral, to be able to tune out the world around you and let yourself experience the moment. To know you're safe letting go..."

"To fly?"

"To soar is a better term, I suppose. It's the trust between two people that allows you to explore without embarrassment or guilt."

"Guilt?"

"Sometimes, sex is about fulfilling each other's needs. Sometimes one person's needs supersede the others. Taking those moments are a gift. I thought Ted and I had a good sex life and to a degree we did. But with Rand I learned sensual and erotic is more of a state of mind, not just physical."

He was quiet while he surveyed the walls, his gaze stopping before a nude sketch of a female. There was no facial expression; just the body and he didn't stop his finger from reaching to touch the line that ran below the model's navel.

"Yes, I'll always have the scars, but time and Rand have helped me put them into perspective."

"Then why no facial features?"

"It's an old sketch, Tom. An exercise my therapist suggested. Draw what my eye saw without the emotion. After a while I learned to become comfortable in my body again. Only then could I add personality to form." She moved away and pulled out several pages stacked on top of each other. Tom moved beside her and was stunned at what he saw. While a similar full body sketch these had features. Her face. As she flipped them from bottom to top, he saw the progression of life come back into her face, saw the scar diminish as her strength overcame the physical reminder.

"You're an amazingly strong-minded woman, Corin. Not many people I know would have the courage to be honest with themselves especially on paper."

"It was a start. I did these for myself, long before I got together with Rand. It was a way to find the other side of the horror of the situation."

"The accident..."

"That too; it was the precursor. Bad enough to lose my mother and child, to be physically broken but to realize my husband had a girl on the side. I never knew, never suspected. I suppose my rose-colored glasses were pretty dense. It was easier not to acknowledge the changes happening in our relationship. I realize now if I'd acknowledged the problem I would have had to deal with it. I didn't know how to correct the problems, wasn't ready to admit I'd failed. When I found out I was pregnant...it was what Ted and I always talked about, what we wanted. And still it wasn't enough; I wasn't enough to satisfy him."

"He was a fool, Corin. He didn't deserve you." She let out a half laugh.

"Do we always get what we truly deserve in this life? And those of us who get it, is it really what we expected? Is the ideal better than the reality?"

"Whoa..." This was a side of her he'd never thought to explore.

"Sorry," she said, turning away from him. "Here, come take a look at these." She pulled a few canvases from the stack and spread them out against the wall. "These were done right after Rand and I got together." He noticed the difference immediately.

"You got your confidence back."

"That too, but more importantly, Rand set me free. He let me just be me, who I was at the moment without judgment or fear of reprisal. It's a gift he gives me every day."

"The freedom to just be yourself?"

"Yes, good and bad." She pulled a different canvas forward and he saw the charcoal sketch of a nude female. There was a horribly visible scar on the model's belly; her haunted expression carried the weight of the trauma. It was a dark portrait, almost sinister.

"This was done right after my divorce came through. I was angry at life and at myself and at anyone who dared to laugh or enjoy their lives around me. I was also on the road to self-destruction. Only after I did this did I realize how low I'd sunk. And I knew only I could change the situation. I've kept it as a reminder of how low I'd allowed myself to sink."

She shuffled through a second stack and pulled another drawing forward. This one was another nude study only while the scar was visible, the facial features were lighter, and more relaxed, accepting. He noted the way she'd drawn her hand, touching the darker line, acknowledging it as a part of herself.

"That was done six months later." She pulled a third canvas forward and he saw just the hint of a smile on the lips of the woman's face. This time it was her face, full and vivid. The scar was still present but not the main focus of the work. "This was done just before I ran into Rand in the Hamptons. I'd finally come to terms with everything that had happened and understood only I could make myself whole."

Tom studied the portrait and understood. "The way I use music and words, you use canvas and paint?"

"Yes, it's my outlet. Like your songs, some are upbeat but I can think of a few ballads that could be considered dark or despondent."

"It's harder to be honest with music, unless you don't care if it has mass appeal."

"Are there songs you've written and not shared

53

with the public or with your partner, Joe? What about with your wives? What makes you know inside it's private and too personal for general consumption?" He smiled and stared.

"Okay, yes, I've written songs nobody will ever hear. Songs that should never have to be heard and should never have been written..." He didn't share with her the catalyst to that thought; instead he turned the focus back. "But you've shared these drawings with me; you've trusted me with this part of you. Somehow I don't think every person you meet gets to see these." He watched her openly and saw a blush creep across her cheeks but she didn't turn away.

"Are you kidding?" Bob's voice came from the doorway and broke the moment. "Even I'm hardly allowed up here and never dare to cross the threshold without an invitation!" Corin and Bob laughed together and the tension eased. While Tom still didn't have an answer to his question of why she shared her work with him he knew this wasn't the time to pursue it.

***

He finished the pizza and walked to the family room, the glass wall calling to him. Outside the ocean seemed calm, relaxed, far from how he felt. He couldn't get the time in her studio out of his mind. After lunch, they'd all headed home with full bellies. Rand had dropped off to sleep on the sofa and Bob was antsy. Finally, Corin took them both to the studio so Rand could nap. It wasn't what Tom expected though he had no real concept of what to expect.

Over the garage, the second floor was bright and airy. Entering the space you came into a small seating area. There were sofas and chairs as well as a small galley kitchen. One door led from either side of the room. Corin didn't offer to take them to the right so he didn't ask. She opened the door to the left and they both moved aside while Bob pushed ahead, anxious to see what was on the easel. Flipping the white cloth back rather unceremoniously he let out an audible gasp.

"Cor, it's wonderful. What made you decide to do this?"

Tom glanced ahead and saw a portrait on the stand. It was probably ninety percent complete, only the background needed additional work.

"Dad's getting older. I wanted him to see I've healed. I'll ship it down before the anniversary." Bob moved towards her and grabbed her in a bear hug.

Tom ignored the tears and whispered words, uncomfortable with their emotions, letting him take in the rest of the canvases in the room. Some were stacked against the wall; others hung haphazardly around the room. Several different styles were represented. The smell of paint permeated the air, as well as the mineral spirits. It was an oddly comforting space even though it was crowded. What caught his attention were the photos tacked to the wall near the portrait. The faces that stared out told him of a contented life, that Corin was a loved child; she'd led a happy life. The woman on the canvas almost seemed to watch him; her mother's likeness all but warned him away from her daughter.

He forced himself to wander away taking in the view from the large expanse of glass on the back wall, her view of the ocean and sky, natural light filtering in. He looked at the other styles of her work. All around him were photographs. Old and new, some framed, some just tacked to an empty patch of wall. Friends, family and Rand watched her work. Her comfort zone he concluded.

Bob's voice was back to booming once again, his crying jag defeated. He was pumping Corin for information on Rand's latest project.

"He's just doing some editing. We'll celebrate in a week or two. Then hopefully we'll take a long vacation someplace warm until spring finds us here."

"What does Rand do?" Tom heard himself ask.

"He's a writer," Corin answered automatically, just as she had yesterday, with no further information. Sheltering him from the mass population, he decided.

"Not just a writer, have you ever heard of the Elliot Rand series?"

Tom was shocked. He'd never associated the two names. There was nothing in the house that would lead you to believe the man was an extremely prolific writer whose latest works were always in high demand.

"Rand is that Elliot Rand? I just figured it was his first name."

"It is. Rand Shepard. Elliot is his pen."

"Jeez, what a group. Famous writers and painters in one household."

"Don't forget about me, I'm Boy Wonder with a computer program."

"And you," Corin added. "You're the musician or should I say 'rock icon!'" She teased him easily and liked his response. Tom couldn't remember the last time he felt his face heat, but Corin had triggered just that response. They stared at each other for a second too long before she turned away and questioned Bob about the portrait.

Taking a second look around he'd spotted the nudes, male and female, felt drawn to both, found himself staring at them. A phone rang in the background and then she joined him. He still didn't know what possessed her to share the intimate works with him. She'd hustled them from the space quickly after Bob's return.

****

He'd returned to the house and flipped channels

on the plasma television, the sound muted so as not to wake Rand. Nothing caught his eye and he shut it off, wandering towards the view. In the distance he watched Corin and Bob at the end of the pier. Whatever they were discussing looked important. He hadn't realized Rand had woken or that he'd moved beside him.

"They smoking?" Rand asked with a yawn and a stretch.

"I...I don't know."

"Probably, she only smokes with Bob when they reminisce. I'll be glad when this damn anniversary is over."

"Anniversary?" Tom asked, playing dumb. Rand's eyes watched him closely.

"The accident, first of this April will be ten years."

"And she lost her mother?" His question shattered his innocence.

"Her too," Rand answered cryptically. A look crossed between them but Rand didn't elaborate, neither did Tom hint at his earlier conversation with Corin. "How about a glass of wine?"

Efficiently changing the subject he wandered away leaving Tom to watch them from the window. Accepting the offered glass, the two men stood side by side, supposedly watching the sun set, yet each knew they were watching the woman who stood on the end of the pier. When the silence grew too heavy Rand finally spoke.

"Bob's a pain in the ass most of the time, but I don't know if Corin would have survived if he hadn't been there for her."

"They're very close."

"Yeah, well, Bob and I have come to a truce. He and Corin burn up the air waves with long phone calls, text messages and e-mails. Deep down they're like brother and sister. Corin's dad and Bob's were brothers. They lived in the same apartment building growing up and were close. I always got the impression Corin was his protector when they were young. After the accident they reversed roles."

"How did you meet?"

"Bob? I met him in Washington, DC then ran into him in Manhattan. He talked me into joining his family for supper." Rand paused to remember and a small smile crossed his lips. "First time I saw her I knew. I fell instantly in love with her. Just seeing her across the room was enough to turn me inside out. She was in the kitchen with a whole group of people, yet she was the only one I saw. I still remember she was wearing jeans and a white man-tailored shirt with a soft buckskin vest. The color was only a shade darker than her hair. I was fixated on the spot. Then she moved her hand and I saw her wedding ring and I knew I had no right to tread on another man's territory."

The situation was eerily similar. Bob bringing him home to family and him falling instantly for the married Corin. The irony of the situation was history repeating itself.

"You knew her when she was married the first time. What happened to her husband?"

There was a protracted silence while Rand swirled the burgundy liquid in his glass. His words were measured but calm. "They both thought it best he moved on after he got his mistress pregnant."

"Ouch," Tom started. "That must have hurt."

"You've no idea, Tom. It wasn't even a year after the accident. Corin was healed physically but emotionally she was still mending. And then Ted knocks up his girlfriend. I didn't like him when we met over that first meal but I figured it was just jealousy. She seemed happy..." He hesitated but added, "If I ever come across that man and Corin's not around, I swear I'll make him sorry for treating her that way. The worst part was she let him go, guilt free."

"Maybe the marriage wasn't working," Tom mused aloud.

"Apparently it was until the accident." Again Rand paused and finally filled in the missing pieces. "Ted swore he didn't care, but in reality I think he got his girlfriend pregnant on purpose. To hurt Corin mostly, pay back for her not being able to have any more."

"Anymore, I didn't realize she had any children." Tom knew he'd be cursed for pumping Rand for information and couldn't help himself. For Corin he'd take his due in hell one day.

"She doesn't. Neither do I, but that's another story. I made a choice early on not to be a parent. With my line of work it didn't seem fair."

"Writing?"

"No, I was military for twenty years, Special Forces. I'd just retired when Corin ran into my car. I'd had my first success with the Elliot Rand series and was looking for a place out at the beach to settle down."

"And..."

"I never wanted the responsibility of a wife and family when I was in the service. When I came out, I saw the world differently. I saw Corin and knew I wanted her for my wife, but I knew I still didn't want to raise kids."

"I've never had any. My second wife wanted to but I could never picture her as a loving mother." Tom didn't share his private decision about birth control.

"Corin would have been a great mother; she's a natural with kids."

"You know I want to ask and don't have the right."

"I agree. I also realize you're attracted to her.

Just remember she's my wife."

"I'm a guest in your home; I wouldn't cross that line, Rand. And Corin hasn't given me the time of day, let alone shown any interest in me other than a guest or friend."

"I know. I trust Corin implicitly. But at times she's still very naive. I'm still a bit surprised she invited you into her studio, but then again, she'd see you as a creative person, only you use notes instead of paint."

"Whereas you use words?" The two men stared at each other before Tom broke the standoff. And that was what it was becoming. A man defending his territory and his wife. Tom knew he had no right to intrude and changed the subject trying to soften the vibe around them.

"What you two have is rare. My partner Joe and his wife Anna are very much like you two. After seeing them together for the past twelve years I came to understand my marriages would never have worked. There was no real trust." The tense air around them defused and Rand shook off his attitude.

"Corin and I have a great life here. Our home is our oasis. We're lucky enough to work on our own schedules and we both still like what we do. Sometimes I think it's all too perfect, someday the other shoe is going to fall and the bottom will drop out."

"If it happens, you and Corin will survive together."

"I have no fear as long as were together, it's when she's alone I worry about." Tom turned quickly to Rand who ignored the unasked question. Finally Tom couldn't hold back his words.

"Rand, are you ill?"

"Not that I'm aware of." He sipped his wine and finished, "I'm ten years older than her; I just meant she'll probably outlive me, statistics and all."

"She's a strong woman in her own right. Let's hope you'll never have to deal with that situation for at least for another thirty or forty years." Rand raised his glass in a toast before draining the liquid.

"They're coming back. I'd prefer our discussion to end here."

"No problem." They both gave curt nods and understood the situation had been clarified from Rand's perspective. For Tom, he accepted the inevitable.

"Good. We'd better get a few more glasses out because the chaos in the kitchen is about to begin, again." Tom realized Rand had shaken off his depressive mood and forced himself to do the same. When Bob and Corin entered, they were chilled and laughing. Bob headed straight for the wine bottle and Corin went right to Rand's side as she tugged off her jacket.

"Pizza time?" she asked.

"Of course," Bob answered. Background music turned into a lesson in the Italian language and love songs and Tom tried not to think about Corin's first husband leaving her after getting another woman pregnant. A fleeting thought went through him that if he ever came across the man, he'd have a few choice words for him too. The rest of the evening went by quickly; growing up in an Italian household came with many stories. Most funny, a few sad, but nobody mentioned the accident. Or the child she'd apparently lost because of it.

Corin talked about some of the masterpieces she'd seen as a child on her first trip there with the family and how it had influenced her creative side. Bob talked about big Sunday get-togethers with lots of food, wine and aunts and uncles all squeezed around someone's kitchen table. Tom got a glimpse of Corin's childhood and refrained from comparing it to his. When they were all sated from the heavenly meal, it was easy to relax in the family room; a fire burning brightly mellowed them all out. Travel plans were coordinated for the morning and one last round of dessert was shared.

That night Tom tried to shut down his mind. Too many thoughts circled around inside and he knew none of them were conducive to sleep. He'd finished his cold pizza and wondered if he'd ever have a home that felt like this. Wondered if he'd ever find a woman to love him the way Corin loved her Rand. The depth of their relationship was staggering. He knew the brief look she'd allowed him into her private side in the studio had been a gift he'd never forget. And probably never return, to her or any woman.

Chapter Five

The scent of chocolate enveloped him, making getting up a necessity. The aroma of coffee wafted past him and he jumped into a quick shower before tossing the last of his stuff into his bag. Corin stood alone in the kitchen, the morning news low in the background. One of her hands held a large baking tray while the other used a thin spatula to slide off the hot chocolate chunk cookies onto a wire rack. Her head popped up when Beau rose for his mandatory head rub, something that had become second nature to Tom.

He'd never had animals growing up; it wasn't that he didn't like them, only they were an added expense to an already tight household budget. When he was on his own, it didn't seem fair to have a pet left behind half the year. But one look at the old hound and he'd lost his heart.

"Morning, coffee's ready and breakfast will be shortly. Did you sleep well?"

Tom paused, waiting for another string of questions and smiled when he didn't get any.

"Good morning to you too. Yes, I'd kill for coffee and I slept like a rock."

"It's the salt air and the sounds of the ocean," she replied, moving about the space with ease. Something was checked in the oven and thick slices of smoked ham were warming in a fry pan. Her movements were practiced and he accepted the second section of the newspaper Rand offered as he joined them. When Bob appeared the meal was ready. A somber affair compared to the others he'd experienced with them.

"You two are going to see each other in June," Rand was saying.

"Maybe before then," Bob added, looking from Rand to Corin. There was a slight silence before Rand continued. He eyed Bob and shook his head in acceptance.

"I've been thinking about taking Corin to Italy for a few weeks in April. The new book is finished, we deserve a vacation."

"You were thinking that?" Corin asked. She seemed surprised and pleased.

"Somewhere else you'd rather go?" He folded the paper section and put it aside.

"No, we haven't been back to Italy since our honeymoon. I like the idea."

"Good, because I've contacted your Uncle Vito and he's assured me there's room at the villa for us."

Corin dropped the dish towel she'd been using and moved quickly towards her husband. Her arm's went around him and hugged him tight. "Thank you. It's a great plan."

"You're welcome. I figured your dad could meet us there for a week or two." She had no words, only the one large tear that ran down her cheek. She buried her face against his shoulder blocking any further emotions she might express. When she pulled back she was smiling at her husband.

"Got it all worked out?"

"Pretty much."

"So it wasn't your editor pushing you to finish the novel," she absorbed.

"Well, her too, but I wanted to have it finished so we could both enjoy some down time." There was a protracted silence where Corin and Rand just watched each other.

"How come I wasn't invited?" Bob chimed in when the silence stretched.

"I don't have to invite you, you just show up!" Corin laughed heartily and the heavy moment passed.

"And I might just do it again. I haven't been to the villa in…God it's got to be seven years."

"Yes, and we didn't invite you then either!" Rand said good-naturedly.

"Well, I gave you a few weeks of privacy first."

"It's a damn good thing you did. I like you Bob, but if you'd shown up any earlier on our honeymoon I'd have had to lock you away in one of the cellars."

"Promises," he tossed back. "You wouldn't lock me away, think of all the wonderful wine you'd miss sampling."

"That too," Rand said, shaking his head. "You're welcome if you can arrange it. Vito's expecting us for the month and already mentioned you'd probably show up."

"What can I say? I need a fix occasionally."

"Give us the first two weeks and join us for the rest of the month."

"Count on it," Bob told him and nobody in the room doubted his word. "But that still doesn't make leaving any easier."

"It's only six weeks away Roberto, I'm sure you'll survive," Rand teased.

"Yeah, I know. But leaving makes me realize what I'm going back to."

"Oh, poor Bob, your town house in Georgetown is such a wreck," Corin added.

"Yes, well. Without you there, it seems pretty boring."

"You'll survive. Besides, you appreciate me more when you're away from me for a few months." Their banter went unnoticed by Rand who buried his nose in the newspaper.

****

An hour later they were ready to leave. The

black bullet as they had all taken to calling it was loaded. His suitcase was in the back and tucked on the front seat was a paper bag Corin had pressed into his hand after a hug good-bye. There were no long last lingering looks or expressions meant for him alone, instead he was simply a guest leaving.

"Just some snacks for the road," she said. "Travel safe, Tom." Her step back beside Rand was as it should have been. He had all their e-mail addresses and phone numbers but still loathed to leave.

"You've been wonderful. Thank you for opening your home to me."

"You're welcome back," Rand started, not surprised when Bob and Corin chorused in, "Any third Sunday!"

He left on a high note with them all smiling, holding a hand up, his fingers crossed as he turned the key. It started with a smooth purr. From the rear view mirror, he watched the same scene repeat a second time with Bob. At the end of the driveway he turned west, heading towards the main road that would take him north towards home. The hollow feeling bothered him most as he drove leisurely along the coast enjoying the treats Corin had sent along. Besides the two sandwiches of turkey and Swiss, layered with spicy mustard, there was an apple and a pear, several paper napkins and a small plastic bag with six of the chocolate chunk cookies she'd baked before breakfast.

****

Trying to be honest with himself, Tom admitted he was alone. Ultimately, the fact was he'd spent his adult life holding people at a distance, never letting anyone get past his defenses to see inside. If they did, they might find the insecurities he hid so well. And most of all they would use the same vulnerability against him.

He'd never let himself completely trust a woman, giving her that last, tangible piece of his trust. And that was why his two marriages never really stood a chance. He was all surface with them, always on alert. He'd loved them and was attracted to them both, but deep inside he knew they were temporary.

The irony of the whole situation wasn't lost on him. A weather delay and a rental car mix up and his life had changed. Not drastically from a physical standpoint. He was going home and getting on with his life as expected. Only now he'd lost his heart to another man's love. He'd felt her in his soul, suddenly believing in true love at first sight. And she barely knew he existed. He understood how Rand felt about her, how protective he was how he'd managed to sequester her away to their oasis where the world didn't intrude.

Tom felt just as protective of her after three days, yet he knew he'd protect her and still show her the world. To see it through her eyes and her painting would truly be a gift in his life. One he'd never see come to fruition. He drove as far as Virginia Beach that night. The truck was handling well and he could have gone further but instead he found himself stopping. In a non-descript hotel room that looked like so many others he'd been in, he savored the last of the cookies, visions of Corin Toscano Shepard on his mind. He pictured her easily wandering the Italian countryside, her hair loose in the breeze. Only the image of Rand walking beside her marred his fantasy. No matter how hard he tried, he couldn't picture himself beside her.

****

Four weeks later Tom tossed his mail onto the side table. There was no note from Corin; the rest of it didn't matter. It wasn't that he was waiting for a thank you, per say, more the contact from her. He'd thought long and hard on the drive home how to thank his hosts for his unplanned stay. The vehicle had become a major hassle since he got back to Boston. Joe and Anna didn't resist teasing him about it. Ultimately, Anna suggested sending steaks they could enjoy when her cousin visited again. He'd gone on-line and placed the order, checking his e-mail until the delivery confirmation came through. Still no contact. Disappointed, he headed to the gym and worked out the aggression he was feeling.

Everyone around him had noticed a change in his behavior but were careful not to mention it directly to him. Mostly when they did his reply was to back off and leave him alone. Anna said in passing one day that he seemed to have lost his heart. He'd given her a deadly look but she'd held his gaze. The silent communication between them was tense and they stayed out of the other's way for a few days. It was a few weeks longer before he got Bob's cryptic e-mail.

"Corin hanging in, but by a thread, so much, so little time. Hope you're well."

"Just what the hell does that mean?" he asked aloud after reading it a second time. Corin hanging in, but by a thread? Without much thought he mailed Bob a reply.

"What the hell is going on and why is Corin hanging in?" Another three days lapsed before he got a call back. Unfortunately, he wasn't there to answer it and Bob left a similar message on his voice mail. Frustrated beyond his means, he called Bob Toscano and was ready for a confrontation. He got the voice mail. Several days passed and he'd stopped checking his mail with regularity. The one thing he wanted to do most was contact Corin; the one thing he knew he couldn't do.

Joe and Anna were over with the girls for a late lunch. The guys had gone over some business details for their upcoming tour while the kids played in his indoor pool. They laughed and swam under the watchful eye of their mother. Anna dropped the mail on the kitchen counter when she went to get the girls a drink, teasing Tom if he'd been corresponding with another man's wife.

Stunned, he pushed back in his seat and forced himself not to run to the pile. Neat black printing presented itself on the outside of the envelope, the return address that of Wilmington Beach, North Carolina. Tom used a butcher knife to slice open the envelope and pulled out the folded note...

"Dear Tom,

I'm sorry for the delay in thanking you for your gifts.

The flowers were lovely and the steaks are waiting for your and Bob's next visit. With everything that's happened in the last weeks it's been hard to keep up.

Please accept my thanks and remember your invitation is always open.

Corin"

He read the note several times, realizing it gave him no real information. That night he called her. Tom didn't care if Rand thought it out of line; instead his gut told him something was wrong. The urge to protect Corin was overwhelming. It had been two months since he and Bob had shown up on their doorstep that rainy night. Two months since he'd slept well or ate normally. Eight weeks he'd managed not to contact her. The postmark was only a few days old which sent up a red flag; she and Rand should have been in Italy by now.

She sounded tired he decided when she picked up the phone. "Hello?"

"Corin, this is Tom Hayden, have I caught you at a bad time?" There was a long pause before she spoke. He felt like a teenager, awkward and unsure of himself. This was so far removed from his normal personality it made him uncomfortable when he thought about it later. That a simple voice on the telephone could unnerve him.

"Tom, how are you?" There was no line of questions following as he'd expected from her.

"I'm fine, Corin, but I'm getting the feeling you're not. Is everything all right down there, you and Rand okay? I got a cryptic e-mail from Bob. Can I help with anything, Corin?" There was a long pause before she answered. It started with a light laugh, low and husky as he remembered.

"I'm not sure which question to answer first or if I remember them all."

"Touché," he answered back, realizing he'd taken to using her running monologue style. "Corin, please tell me what's going on."

"Tom this is extraordinarily hard for me to say."

"Corin, what's happened?" He heard her take several deep measured breaths before answering. "Rand passed away," was all she managed to get out before she had to stifle a sob. The pregnant pause over the dead air waves was thick with dread.

"Passed away, but how, when?" His voice had lowered his words for his own comprehension more than her answers.

"The end of March. He was out jogging and had a heart attack."

"My God, Corin," was all he managed to get out in response until he forced himself to remember their situation. "I'm so sorry, is there anything I can do to help?"

"No thanks. Family and friends here have been wonderful. Bob came down for a week and my father was here for a while. He just headed home a few weeks ago."

"I'm so sorry, Corin. I know how much you loved him, how he loved you."

"Yes, we loved each other very much."

"How can I help?"

"There's really nothing that can be done, Tom, although I appreciate your offer."

"Why didn't you call and let me know, or Bob, why didn't he call?"

"We knew you were just getting the tour started again and there wasn't anything anyone could do. It was just too late."

****

The rest of the conversation went quickly, Tom not knowing what to say. He made her promise to keep in contact with him and told her he'd try to see her when the tour was in her area. She was polite yet distant. His next call was to Bob whom he finally reached. With his voice just a hair under hollering he got Bob's attention quickly.

"Why the hell didn't you call me, or at least get me a message?" There was no need to elaborate they both knew exactly what he meant.

"Hello, to you too, Tom, and what did you expect me to do, call you so you could come running down to take his place?" Stunned, Tom lost all his anger. "I mentioned it and she said not to bother you. Besides, she needs time to mourn her loss."

"I understand that, I'm not a complete moron, but I could have helped, somehow."

"No, you would only have confused the issue. I know you're in love with her, Tom, there's no hiding that. But she needs time and space to accept her husband is gone before getting romantically or sexually involved with another man."

"What kind of a man do you think I am, that I'd hit on her at his funeral?"

"You wouldn't have to hit on her; just your presence would have been..."

"Been what?"

"Distracting."

71

"Was I that obvious?" Tom questioned, accepting his behavior hadn't gone unnoticed.

"Not really, but Corin doesn't take many people into her studio. And she's never shown her nudes that I'm aware of. Of course Rand had seen them and me." Bob cleared his throat before continuing. "That day in her studio, Tom, she gave you a bit of herself. I'm not sure if she realized she was doing it herself. Only it was natural to share them with you. She won't question why she did unless you push her and she won't acknowledge the attraction, won't deal with it for a while, if ever. And you can't push her. Corin deserves to decide in her own time frame."

Tom ran his fingers through his hair and rubbed his eyes. "Is she all right, Bob?"

"Yes and no. She's not suicidal but she's deeply saddened. She and Rand had a bond, Tom. Their love was very rare, but you realized that yourself."

"Yes, he was her safe place."

"That too, they had a connection that was more than physical; it was spiritual in an abstract sort of way."

"What actually happened?"

"He went for a jog one afternoon and didn't come home. Just about the time she realized he'd been gone too long the sheriff showed up. He'd collapsed a few blocks away. It was just too late for help. Afterwards, the autopsy revealed he'd had a congenital heart defect that was never caught."

"My God, that weekend he was so alive..."

"And..."

Tom finally put the pieces together as a wave of nausea passed through him. "And you're going to tell me he died at the time of her accident."

"A week before, yes."

"Jeez, how is the woman supposed to live through April next year?" It was a rhetorical question. "I figured they'd be in Italy about now."

Neither man felt the need to elaborate; the silence that passed was welcomed.

"Just give her some time, Tom. Let her grieve. Maybe in the summer give her a call, check in on her."

"Wait until summer," he mused. Bob let out a small laugh.

"Yes, at least summer. You're a big strong man, you can do it!"

"Yeah, I can. But I don't have to like it."

"Look at it from this perspective. If she were your wife would you want him calling weeks after you were in the ground to 'check on her'?"

"Put that way...but it still sucks. You'll keep me posted?"

"If you like, are you sure Tom? I love Corin to death; I don't want to see her hurt."

"I'm not looking for a new conquest, Bob. I truly care about her, for God's sake; I did fall in love with her that weekend. Is that what you want to hear?"

"Close enough. I suppose you might make an all right brother-in-law, but not for a while, Tom. I'll keep you updated."

"Thanks. How are you holding up, she told me you went down for a week?"

"It was an awful time, Tom. A beautiful funeral if there is such a thing, but an awful time. Her dad came up too and between Rand dying and the anniversary..."

"Bob..."

"I'll call in a few weeks, Tom. Good luck with the tour. I've got to go."

"All right, thanks Bob. And thanks for being there for her."

"Damn, you sounded like Rand just then. I'm always there for her as long as I'm alive."

"Let's just keep it that way, all right?"

"Yeah, well it's my projected outcome too."

As he disconnected the phone, Tom whispered, "That was Rand's plan too."

Stunned, Tom wandered through his house in the darkness realizing how many times he'd said something similar. Next month, next year, when I retire. Overwhelmed, he tried to put Rand and especially Corin out of his mind. The harder he tried, the more she became imbedded in his soul. Bob's words about her sharing a piece of herself with him stayed prominent and gave him some hope for the future. Tom knew that future would be far off in the distance, if ever.

Chapter Six

Tom Hayden was living his life just going through the motions. Each day he did what he was supposed to when he was supposed to and each day he was preoccupied with thoughts of Corin. He'd called seven galleries in Soho before he found the one Corin shipped her works to, only to be told they didn't have any left. The polite female voice on the other end of the telephone offered to call him if any more came in but he decided that wouldn't be a good idea.

At the end of June he lost all restraint. On a rainy summer night he broke down and actually let the call go through. When he realized it rang it was too late to hang up, his hands went clammy and his stomach unsettled. She answered too quickly.

"Hello?"

"Corin," he managed to whisper, forcing himself to take a breath.

"Who is this?"

"It's Tom Hayden, Corin. Did I get you at a bad time?" He would have liked to have seen her face when she recognized her caller. It would set the tone for the rest of the conversation. Instead he was flying blind.

"Tom, how's the tour going?" At least she remembered him that was a plus.

"Typical. It's fine. How are you doing Corin?"

"Fine Tom, really I'm okay." Her answer was too quick, her voice too trained. He waited several seconds before laughing lightly, unable to hold it back.

"All right, we got that out of the way, how about you tell me what level of horrible it's been instead?" At first he was afraid he'd gone too far, been to bold until she spoke.

"All right, it sucks. I'm so tired of being depressed and maudlin."

She let out a resigned sigh and Tom knew he loved her. He knew for his own peace of mind he had to tell her, somehow, without crossing the imaginary line he never could see.

"Corin, I've thought about you often and wanted to call more times than I care to admit, you've not been out of my mind. I know you needed some time and space, but I want you to understand I'm here for you, when you're ready."

Great, he thought, he'd just all but told her he was desperately in love with her and all he was getting was dead air. "I'm not pushing; I just want you to realize you're not alone."

"I don't know what to say, I'm a little taken aback Tom."

"I'm not trying to confuse you, Corin, just know I'm here if you need me." Another protracted silence and he got nervous, afraid he'd blown it. Instead, he tried to change the subject. "Tell me about your cousin's wedding. Did she really look like a meringue and did Bob tell her to her face?"

"Yes and almost," she finally answered. "She looked lovely, just a little fluffy and Bob was on his best behavior." Hesitating, she added, "It was difficult to get through, Tom."

"But you went anyway..."

"It wasn't about me; it was about her and her dreams of the future and celebrating the beginning of a new life together."

"I give you a lot of credit, Corin. I'm not sure if I were in your position I'd of made it through the day without..."

"Breaking down? Well, I did have a few of those moments, but Bob stayed close. I had to go, Tom. Better to let the family see I'm not defeated by losing Rand, only saddened."

****

Corin realized the moment was getting much too heavy and with a laugh told him several funny stories relating to the party. A ring bearer who refused to relinquish the golden circles entrusted to him, an uncle who drank too much and hit on the groom's mother. The bride's bouquet getting stuck in the chandelier when she tossed it. All a diversion to her true feelings and emotions she wanted to share with this man and couldn't.

"Corin, did your dad like the portrait of your mother?"

"Yes, he did."

"Have you started one of Rand?"

"No."

"It's too soon, isn't it?"

"Yes," was all she managed.

"All right, Corin, I'll keep in touch. You know how to get hold of me if you need anything, use the cell phone or e-mail."

"Thanks Tom." She hung up quickly and decided not to read too much into the situation. He was just a nice man who probably felt obligated in a small way. She'd probably never hear from him again.

And just as well. Tom Hayden was a distraction she didn't need. Corin's goal was to find herself again and a path she was comfortable with. So far, since losing Rand, peace was elusive, pain prominent. Deep inside, she knew there was nothing she could do about the grief; only try to live through it.

****

Actually thankful a hurricane was brewing off the African coast line, Tom used it as an excuse to call Corin near the end of July. If she'd seen through his motives she didn't let on, instead she allayed his fears easily and they fell into a conversation centering more on his touring than Corin and her situation.

With each storm he called her, becoming only slightly obsessive about checking the weather reports no matter where he was. Any excuse to call her was used. When the fourth storm was projected she answered the phone laughing.

"It's only a tropical storm," she said, her voice light for the first time in months.

"I know," he said, "but it was an excuse to call."

"Do you need excuses, Tom?"

"I felt I did, are we past that now?" For long moments neither said a word, accepting it had to be her decision.

"I don't think you need excuses to call me." Tom was slightly stunned by her words.

Tom was not only surprised by her answer but also the conversation that followed. Brutally honest from the start with him, she wasn't looking to replace Rand, nor was she looking for a relationship of any kind at this point in her life. She quickly reminded him she'd only been a widow for six months.

But she was also honest enough to tell him she'd come to look forward to his calls. And she wasn't sure if that was good or bad at this point. Only when she admitted to him that she wasn't sure why she invited him into the studio that day did he relax. At least she was thinking about him. They decided easily they'd both know if it turned wrong.

****

August was his best month since first meeting and falling in love, then leaving behind another man's wife. They spoke several times a week, Tom calling every second or third day and Corin initiating a call occasionally. When she did phone him it was always with a funny tidbit about life in general or something Bob did. He'd grown to look forward to their talks and found himself opening up to her more each time. She too was giving him glimpses into her past.

Occasionally she mentioned Rand and he tried not to sound jaded. She'd been going through the stages of loss, but was still holding onto a lot of anger. At Rand, at herself and at the powers above that had let it happen. He tried to listen and not give pat answers when he had no real words to comfort her. Letting her vent was the best he could do.

He mentioned the possibilities of getting to see her in the near future but she didn't jump at his offer. He backed off, hoping it was the right thing to do.

****

Which brought them back to square one, right here and right now. With hurricane Iris swirling up the coast towards Corin. She was being stubborn and pigheaded, refusing to leave her home. He'd blown it, he knew, ordering her to abandon her house. But from his perspective it was the smart thing to do. Emotions aside, he wanted her safe, and if that meant with him, so be it. Only she wasn't adapting to his plan. Frustrated, he wanted to slam the phone into the hotel wall.

He resigned himself to being stuck a state away riding out the storm. The hot shower didn't help, neither did the beer. Food had no taste. He didn't sleep that night; he kept the weather channel on, constantly monitoring Iris' progress. They were supposed to perform Friday and Saturday nights, a reality that wasn't going to happen leaving him even more frustrated. Stuck back in Virginia Beach, he'd hoped to talk her into coming up to see him and the show. Instead, Iris had banished all talk of Corin taking a leisurely trip up the coast.

Friday dawned cold and grey with heavy rain. Everyone was stuck at the hotel with not much to do. While the storm was predicted to pass the Virginia coast far enough out to sea not to bother them with more than heavy wind and rains, most businesses were prepared just in case. In the past this would have been a minor inconvenience, the shows re-scheduled and they'd wait out the bad weather.

This storm was different. Tom felt useless in more ways than he preferred to count. He spent most of the day in front of the television changing channels for the latest reports. The rest of the time he spent on the phone trying to make arrangements to get to Wrightsville Beach. Renting a vehicle was almost impossible, let alone the truck of his choice. The rest of the time he spent tinkering with the composition of Another Man's Love. He hadn't even played it for Joe yet. He'd kept the words and melody to himself, unwilling to share them with anyone just yet.

"We were never supposed to meet.
Fate has its way.
She's everything I ever wanted,
But dared not dream.
She's another man's love,
She doesn't notice me.
She's another man's love,
She'll never be free."

That was where the song stalled. Since learning about Rand's death he hadn't wanted to take the song in any direction, hoping time would unravel it. Only now, the words sounded different in his head. Instead of the ballad being about something you can't ever have, maybe it would be about the possibilities. Thinking it around in circles just gave him a headache and he gave up trying. History taught him most things happened in their own time.

After eight that night he knocked on Joe's door. Anna opened it with a smile and moved to let him in.

"Are you as bored as we are?" she asked.

"Just antsy," he answered automatically. "You're missing the girls."

"That too, two weeks with them up at Mom's sounded good last May when we made the arrangements, now I'm missing them like crazy." She dropped next to her husband who was stretched out on the bed, several national newspapers scattered around him. Joe looked up and waited for Tom to tell them what was on his mind.

"I'm leaving early in the morning," he started. "I've managed to rent a truck with four wheel drive and am heading down the coast." He let out the breath he'd been holding since his hand reached their door. Moving to the sliding glass door, he pulled the curtain further back, watching the copious amounts of rain.

"Is she all right?" Anna asked.

"Last I heard, yes. But that was late last night. I didn't have the guts to call her this morning and now I can't get a line through."

"Why not?" Joe asked, confused by his long time partner's apprehension.

"Because I basically pissed her off, all but ordering her to drive up here to ride out the storm." Joe's head just nodded and Anna's eyes widened.

"You ordered her up here?" she said, not believing him.

"I didn't mean it that way; I just wanted her to be safe."

"But it came out as an order not a request?" She managed to hold back her smile when his fingers rubbed his aching temples. "And today, you didn't try?"

"She's not answering her cell, the land lines are

down."

"The battery's probably dead," Joe offered. "Power's down all over, she just didn't get to re-charge it."

"Thanks," Tom answered with a half laugh.

"Want company?" Anna asked, sitting up as she tried to appraise the situation.

"Yeah, I do, actually, if you don't mind a long drive and not knowing what's going to be on the other end."

"I'm game," Joe offered.

"Me too, anything to get us out of this room." Anna smiled at Tom and he winked. They'd been around each other long enough to understand each other without saying all the words. If Joe was like a brother, Anna was like a sister.

"I don't know what the situation will be..."

"Better we're all together, then. When do you want to leave?"

"As early as possible, the rental agency promised to deliver the truck here by eight." Anna nodded and told him they'd be ready. "I'm not sure what kind of trip this is going to turn into," he offered once again but Joe finished for him.

"We'll figure out a way to get to her, Tom. Get some sleep; it's going to be a long drive."

"Thanks, see you in the morning."

****

For the rest of the night different stations gave varying reports of damage through out the coastal area from South Carolina up to Virginia Beach. Iris it seemed had made landfall only slightly further down the coast of North Carolina. That would mean Corin should have gotten hit with just the fringes of the storm. But he really had no way of knowing. After eleven he jumped into a hot shower, thankful once again the hotel had invested in massive back-up generators. It wasn't until much later when he was turning out the light he noticed he had a voice message.

"Tom, it's Corin, I just wanted to let you know I'm all right. We've had some damage, and the tide is still in. Mostly it seems just downed trees and debris but the house and Beau are all right."

That was it. She'd called when he was in the shower and now it was too late to call her back. Maybe it was better this way, if he spoke to her tonight he'd have no real reason to drive down to check on her. He slept, but fitfully; he had odd dreams of cold dank places. He awoke before dawn to find out Iris had blown out to sea and it looked like it was going to be a beautiful day for clean up and repairs. He hoped so, or it was going to be an even longer drive south.

****

They encountered problems with their trek. Some of the smaller towns and hamlets were worse off than others. The path of the storm had followed the coast, leaving fits of damage in odd spurts. Some places looked virtually untouched while others would take months to be put right. Most businesses were closed, only the odd gas station or fast food restaurant was open. There were no traffic lights in some places and the few shopping centers they passed seemed closed except for the home improvement centers. Their parking lots were packed.

There were a few moments when he was afraid they wouldn't make it to Corin's. They were detoured numerous times around downed power lines and trees. It was nearing late afternoon when he finally hit the secondary road leading them to her.

Apprehension churned inside him as he made the turn into her driveway. The long winding path was beyond rutted. Narrowed in spots from trees and limbs, water pooled in odd places. Someone had been there earlier in the day they realized, seeing several trees had been moved from their path, chunks of wood tossed to the side for later cutting as firewood. As they hit the rise of the driveway Tom slowed the truck, unsure of what he was really seeing.

Anna said the words out loud. "Is that your Corin on the roof?"

Her question was probably more for herself than for Tom but it was valid when verbalized.

"Son of a bitch!" he hissed through his teeth as he forced the truck up the muddy road, not caring if he was doing more damage to the path. He spun it to a stop before the garage and was about to bolt from behind the steering wheel.

Joe grabbed his sleeve and forced him to look at him.

"Take a breath, Tom," was all he managed to get out before Tom jumped out, his strong legs taking long angry strides towards the side of the building where an aluminum extension ladder was propped. Beau watched him come closer and let out a few low howling sounds before Tom spoke.

"It's all right, Beau. You remember me, boy," he said as the dog approached. Once he'd gotten his head and ears quickly petted he moved onto the next human who might show him some attention. Tom took long hard breaths forcing air into his lungs, hoping the spinning in his head would stop.

"Damn it, Corin, get down from there!" All right, he knew it wasn't the best opening statement he could have used, but it was what was on his mind.

"Hello to you too, Tom, nice of you to drop by." She put the hammer down and sat carefully beside the blue tarp she'd stretched over that portion of the roof. He noted both windows were intact and was thankful for that. They held each other's look for long seconds before Anna approached, breaking the stand off.

****

Corin had seen the vehicle coming up the drive and didn't have a clue as to who was inside. Not that it really mattered. Whoever it was had good intentions, she decided, knowing how many calls and drop by's she'd received today. Acknowledging it was Tom Hayden in this vehicle made her go all soft and tingly. Not the front she wanted to present. While wanting nothing more than to have him hold her against his solid body, she knew she had to stand her ground, or roof as it were. She was aware there were more people in the vehicle but her attention was trained on Tom. It annoyed her that she'd missed him, pissed her off that she desired him. She'd realized he'd been on her mind a lot lately, too much, she decided just one day last week when she found herself sketching his profile.

Tom would have no way of knowing how much courage it took for her to make the call last night. Corin knew she was opening a door to him and wondered if he'd walk through it now that his bluff had been called. Deep in the back of her mind he was there, haunting her with each task she encountered. There were definitely emotions attached to her thoughts, ones that thrilled and scared her. Corin had fallen in love with Tom Hayden.

Differently than she'd loved and desired Rand, but it was a definite feeling inside her; she knew she was falling for Tom. And now, after all this time he'd found her nailing tarps to the garage in old coveralls, Rand's old flannel shirt and work boots with her hair blowing wildly in the soft winds. She cursed herself for the snap decision to cut it short.

"Hello, I'm Anna Haas; this is my husband, Joe."

"Hello, Anna, Joe, welcome to the beach." Corin bit back a laugh with her words, as if they were standing on her front porch, not separated by two stories of building. "I'll be down in just a minute; I've only a few nails to finish this. I'm glad you all stopped by, I could use a break."

She carefully stood and moved back to the two by four she was using to hold down the tarp. While she nailed it down, she kept talking. "How was your trip down? Were the roads a mess? Were there many detours? How does the rest of Wilmington look, I haven't been out yet. When was the last time you had anything to eat or drink?"

Tom's voice bellowed above hers. "Damn it, Corin, get down from the roof!"

She paused deciding how to handle him, and her new guests. "I will Tom, as soon as this is finished. Then I won't have to climb back up." She turned her back on them and heard him rattle off a stream of curse words directed towards her stubborn nature, the garage roof, the storm and her inability to listen.

With that one she took exception and paused, slowly turning her attention back.

"What did you expect me to do, Tom? Leave it open to the elements? My studio is below this spot." Her look dared him to refute her words or their meaning.

"Damn it, Corin, you could get hurt up there. Wasn't there some man you could have called if it was so important and couldn't wait?" With no elaborate gasp or pause, Corin simply turned her back on him.

Tom walked away muttering to himself, apparently not caring that he was slogging through the thick layer of mud her back yard had turned into. It took all her strength not to holler back she'd already gotten hurt up here and was scared to death but didn't see any other options. Having it thrown in her face stung. When he'd gone, Corin turned back to her guests.

"I'm about ready for a glass of lemonade, how about you?" Joe and Anna both noticed how carefully she moved above them, they obviously saw how frightened she truly was. After some discussion, they moved to the side while she tossed down her hammer and a few spare pieces of lumber. Joe steadied the ladder as she came down, kind enough not to mention he saw her knuckles whiten with each rung she descended. When she finally hit ground, she turned and smiled to them, welcoming them both.

Anna defused the situation further.

"You must tell me how you manage to rile him up so easily?" All three of them waited about three seconds before bursting out laughing. Joe shook his head and wandered towards the ocean where his friend stood with his back to them.

"Come inside, we'll talk," Corin said, somehow liking this woman before she even got to know her. At least she spoke her mind, something Corin did with regularity, even when it would have been better to remain silent.

Chapter Seven

Corin's shoulder hurt. It was sore and should be washed but she refused to let on she was injured, even slightly. Bustling around her kitchen she easily set the coffee to drip while she pulled out tins of homemade cookies. She and Anna were putting out mugs and plates when the two men entered the house through the back door, both stopping to toe off their muddy boots.

"You guys are just in time," Corin said, hoping her voice was steady. "Come and have a seat," she continued, refusing to let her eyes meet Tom's. He moved towards the sink and made a production of washing his hands while Joe and Anna discussed the various stages of destruction they'd passed along the way. Corin began to tell them about some missing siding and roof shingles when she felt Tom's eyes boring through her.

Without turning, she added she'd already called the contractor to get on his repair list. Nobody took the thread of conversation further; Anna mentioned the picture over the fireplace and changed the subject.

"I'd love to see the rest of your work," Anna was saying when Tom turned to watch the scene unfolding before him.

"Thanks," he managed as she passed him a hand towel, his anger not quite in check.

"You're welcome," she smiled and moved back to the refrigerator pulling out chunks of cheese that kept her busy slicing and arranging plates. When she moved past him to the pantry she wondered absently if he'd follow. A vision of her and Rand in there came to mind and she dismissed all thoughts of Rand or Tom in the pantry.

While she opened crackers, Corin keep a running commentary about the storm going with Anna and Joe. When she'd set out snacks she finally ran out of steam, dropping onto the bar stool across from his friends.

For a long time Tom hesitated to take the seat beside her. Corin wondered if he hesitated because it was Rand's seat, his place. Rand was dead yet he was still alive around them in this space. She saw reluctance on his face as he grabbed the glass carafe and refilled everyone's mugs before moving to sit beside her.

His hand went to her shoulder as his words spilled out. "I'm sorry I yelled, Corin," was all he got out. The minute he touched her shoulder she let out a small groan and tried to pull away. Joe and Anna sat wide eyed as Tom's finger's pulled at the neckline of the flannel shirt she wore. With one tug he'd effectively bared her shoulder, her scraped and bruised shoulder and upper arm. At the same time Corin twisted away from him and pulled her shirt back in place.

"Damn it, Corin, you did get hurt!" Tom lowered his voice and dropped his hand from her arm.

"*Yes!*" she shouted back. "I got hurt. Are you happy now! I went up there and slipped. But it's only a scratch and I survived. Now tell me you were right, go ahead, you were." Hazel eyes bored through hers glaring back, daring him to open his mouth. "Nothing comes to mind or too many to choose? Well? Could we just let it go?" The staring contest continued and Corin realized he wouldn't back down.

"No," he gritted out. "Just how crazy are you? What in God's name made you climb up two stories to cover that blasted roof?" They stood toe to toe with neither giving quarter. While Corin was at least eight inches shorter than Tom her attitude made up the difference. Eye to eye they strained until Corin broke the moment.

****

"You're right. I shouldn't have gone up there. I saw no other choice. It had to be done or the studio would have been damaged further." She waited for him to answer and when he didn't Anna interceded.

"Was there a lot of damage, Corin?" Defused temporarily, she shook off her anger and resentment and turned back to Anna.

"Some, I managed to move most of the canvases late last night." Nobody dared to ask aloud how she got to the garage with the tide still in.

"If you need a hand getting it cleaned up…"

"Thanks." She took several breaths before adding, "If you'll excuse me for a few minutes, I'm going to jump in a quick shower. I'm head to toe sawdust after this morning."

"You cut the trees down?" Joe asked before thinking.

"No," she said with a weak smile. "Some neighbors dropped by early this morning and helped me clear them. I just served cookies and thanked them."

Tom let out an odd snort-like sound and Corin refused to acknowledge it.

"My friends and neighbors have been great, but they all have work to do on their own homes and businesses." She turned to Tom before adding, "Please make Anna and Joe comfortable. You pretty much know where things are around here." Heading to the hallway she turned back, "I'll just be a few minutes and then we'll see about supper."

"We were going to take you out to eat," Anna started to say.

"I appreciate that, maybe tomorrow. I doubt

there's much open tonight. Once the power comes back on things will get back to normal. Besides, it's been a long day for all of us, I'm sure the ride down wasn't as easy as you're making it sound. Let's just all relax and regroup." Her words carried many meanings and nobody tried to define them aloud.

****

Beau followed her as she disappeared from the kitchen. Nobody in the kitchen said a word for a long time; Tom knew they were watching him. Finally he conceded.

"All right, I'm an ass. I shouldn't have hollered at her."

"Seems to me you're telling the wrong person," Joe said, leaving the counter and heading to the family room. He flipped on the television and scanned channels until Anna joined him, studying the painting with renewed interest. Tom found himself dropping plates and mugs into the dishwasher and washing out the coffee pot. It struck him that he'd never washed a dish or cleared a table his whole adult life, until he'd met Corin. Now it was automatic, just like enjoying leftovers.

A quick glance told him Anna and Joe were settled on the sofa, apparently discussing Corin's painting. Tom used the time to slip from the room and head upstairs. She'd put him in the same guest room he'd used the last time he was here and Joe and Anna were in the room Bob had used. He hesitated at the top of the stairs and again at her bedroom door.

It was ajar and he could see inside for the first time. Directly in front of him was a seating area with another large stone fireplace. Beau was stretched on the wood floor before it. The area rug was rolled up in front of a butter colored suede sofa that was stacked with pictures and other decorating items. The walls glinted back, the paint fresh. He could hear her moving in the other room and reluctantly knocked on the inside door. Corin opened it as she used a towel to dry her hair. She'd pulled on clean, threadbare jeans and a tank top but was barefoot.

"Yeah," she started but stopped short seeing Tom standing in the doorway.

He gave himself the time to give her a complete head to toe stare, knowing from the blush creeping onto her cheeks it was rude. His stare came back to her shoulder and arm.

"Got anything to put on that?" he ventured, not moving into her private space.

She studied him carefully before nodding and then turned but didn't tell or ask him to follow. He did anyway and was surprised when he moved into the bedroom. It too was torn apart. The mattress and box spring were pulled to the center of the room and the smell of fresh paint assaulted him immediately. The walls were a soft green with a hint of blue, the exact opposite of the sitting room. The windows were bare. Obviously she was changing the space and he wondered what it had looked like before. Corin paused in the doorway to the master bath and watched him before acknowledging what he saw.

"I had to change it. I couldn't sleep in here the way it was." Her statement made, he heard her rummaging in the bath. When she looked up he was watching her from the threshold, taking in the white marble bathroom.

The walls above the ceramic tile and marble were painted a light blue that softened towards the ceiling line where white billowing clouds were roughed in, waiting for their final layers of color. He noticed there were several cans of paint in the cloth covered whirlpool bath tub. Stacked alongside were paint brushes and several odd-looking sponges.

He took the tube from her fingers and gently started to apply the ointment. Neither said a word, but their eyes didn't leave the mirror in front of them. At one point he felt and watched her wince. His free hand came up to her other shoulder and held her in place.

"Almost done," he whispered. As if the words gave him courage he continued. "I spent all day watching that stupid storm, the phone within reach and you call the few minutes I decide to jump in a shower."

"Timing's everything…" she ventured, unsure of her voice.

"I know. Thank you for calling back."

In a steadier voice she said, "I didn't want you to worry," but averted her eyes from his. His fingers held her still but refrained from pulling her body back against his chest.

When he looked back in the mirror and saw the two of them standing there it was overwhelming, how she looked with him, how right he felt to her. He finally cleared his throat and broke the tension.

"Thanks," she managed to utter when he recapped the tube and slipped it into her hand. She didn't move and neither did he.

"I'm sorry. I have no right to holler at you or second-guess you. But, Corin, if you'd seen yourself balancing up there from my perspective…you scared the hell out of me."

Still watching in the mirror she didn't turn away. "You think you were scared…," she started then burst into tears, turning into his waiting arms, burying her head against his shoulder.

He let her cry out her anger and hostility until she slowly composed herself. Who was he kidding; he was holding her because he wanted to feel her against him.

Moving from him she managed to grab tissues

and dry her eyes. "Sorry," she started, then stopped when she saw the look on his face.

"Please, promise me you won't go back up there."

"I promise. It wasn't my first choice, just a necessity."

"You're exhausted," he started, knowing he was staring. "And you cut your hair." His fingers threaded through her short, damp, chin length curls, feeling the soft texture sift through his fingers.

"I know," she said back, answering both his statements. "It's better to be exhausted, at least that way I'm numb. Time moves quicker."

"Is that why you're painting your bedroom?"

"More like reclaiming it, making it my own. It's the first real step toward change I've been able to make."

"That's progress at least." She nodded but didn't move away.

"Corin...we're still in his space." She accepted his answer, somewhat surprised he understood. "Someday soon, I'm going to get you alone and away from here and then I won't be able to hold back. Do you understand me, Corin?"

"Yes, I do. But I appreciate you understanding about Rand's presence here."

"It was his home with you, not mine. It never will be."

"I know that too. I also know it won't ever be just mine." The cryptic look she gave him made him realize she was doing a lot of thinking on her own.

"Things are as settled as they can get for a while here, drive back to Virginia with us and spend a few days away from here."

"I can't. Not now, there's too much to do. Insurance adjusters, clean up crews, the trees have to be cut into firewood and stacked, and no, I've already talked to the boys next door. They'll do it, but I need to oversee it all."

He let out a resigned sigh, "All right, for now. I'll give you some time, Corin, but I want to spend some time with you, alone and away from here. Can you understand that?"

"Yes, I'm just not ready yet. And to be honest I'm not sure when I will be. It could take a long time, Tom. I think it's best if you moved ahead with your life."

"Since the third Sunday in February I've been trying to do just that and it's not working. If Rand hadn't passed away I would have been forced to, but he did and I can't get past you. I've tried." Her facial expression gave away the tension she felt. "Too much, too soon, I know. But when you finally realize you've put Rand in perspective, I'll be waiting."

She didn't give him the answer he wanted or expected.

"We have company downstairs and I have supper to start." She moved past him and grabbed a white man-tailored shirt from the bed, pulling it on as she left the room.

By the time he rejoined them downstairs, they were already into the throes of meal preparation, Corin explaining they had electricity because of a backup propane generator system they'd installed during the renovation. The system dominated the conversation as she defrosted homemade tomato sauce in the microwave while pasta water boiled. Anna sliced a loaf of fresh bread then slathered it with a buttery garlic mixture. Joe was opening a bottle of wine when Tom moved into the group, retrieving glasses for them all. He was thankful when Corin asked him to set the dining table in the small breakfast area of the windowed alcove off the living room.

****

The meal went easily, conversation centering on Anna and Joe's daughters, the tour, the new album, anything but the one thing Tom wanted to hear. He knew she wouldn't talk to him in front of his friends and was thankful, even if he was slightly frustrated. He knew sooner or later, before he left, he'd take her aside and have his talk. For now, he was content to be with her in a warm inviting space. The sauce she'd put together was wonderful, spicy and flavorful with the sweet sausage. The salad and garlic bread disappeared quickly.

When they were finishing up, several friends stopped by. Two of the visitors Tom had met on his last trip. Neither seemed overly surprised to see him there or at least they didn't say it to his face. More pots of coffee were consumed as well as more cookies and an apple Danish that all but melted in his mouth. All the conversation centered on the storm and damage left behind. He'd caught a bit of one conversation and Corin assured her counterpart that she'd look in on two neighbors the next day.

****

Corin was taking the last batch of cookies from the oven when the phone rang. With it tucked between her shoulder and chin, she didn't miss a beat sliding the morsels onto cooling racks. Anna sat at the other end of the counter wrapping cooled cookies in cellophane. Tomorrow they would head into town and deliver all the goodies she'd been baking since the storm hit. The local news coverage made them all realize how lucky Corin and her home had been. Just a few miles south the storm had been much more unforgiving. Several shelters had been set up and already the Red Cross was on site to help. After several minutes she hung up the phone.

"Sorry, my Dad's down in Florida, just checking in." No sooner had she dropped it onto the counter and it rang again. "Hello?"

Tom moved back to the kitchen, restless before the television. He sneaked one of the cooling cookies and Anna just laughed. "I'm fine, really. The yard is a mess but nothing too drastic and I haven't had the guts to pull back the pool cover. I've got three extra sets of hands to help, but it's still too wet out to really attempt a clean up." She laughed several times before he heard the hesitation in her voice. "Actually, you do know my guests, but then again you know just about everyone I do!"

Instantly, Tom knew she was talking to Bob.

"No, wrong again. Tom Hayden came down along with his partner Joe and his wife Anna." He glanced to see her facial expression but her back was to him. "I'll ask, hold on," she turned to Tom before extending the phone. "It's Bob, want to say hello?"

"Sure," he answered automatically, popping the last bite of cookie into his mouth before reaching for the phone.

"Hang on Bob; I'll give the phone to Tom. I'll call you tomorrow night to check in." Corin extended her hand then pulled it back, using her fingers to cover the mouth piece, forcing Tom to question her move. "Don't you dare tell..." He and Anna watched her control her attitude before she continued. "Please don't tell him about the garage roof."

Thrusting the plastic piece towards him she left the room.

****

Tom knew Bob wouldn't be happy he was there with Corin for any reason. "Hey, Bob, how's it going?" He tried to sound nonchalant. "What's going on in DC?"

"What am I doing? What the hell are you doing?"

"Relax, Bob. Our shows were canceled in Virginia Beach, we decided to drive down and see if we could lend a hand. Unfortunately, as Corin told you, it's too wet to really get much done." It sounded plausible if you didn't over think it.

"Somehow I'm sure raking her back yard wasn't

your ulterior motive for the trip."

"Of course it was...," Tom started and couldn't finish the sentence.

"Is she really all right, the house is intact?"

"Yeah, pretty much. She lost some siding and some roof shingles, but she said she already spoke with the contractor and the insurance company," he relayed.

"Well that makes me feel better, somewhat. I assume that the back up system is running since you have power?"

"Yeah, that's quite a set up she's got out there."

"Expensive, but worth it. There was a long debate about how often it would get used but ultimately they decided it would be worth it. I don't want to think about her schlepping gas cans up those stairs to a portable generator to keep that place running. The freezers and refrigerator alone would have it running all day, not to mention the water pump and hot water heater."

"Yeah, it's a whole different way of life than I'm used to."

"So is Corin." Bob didn't pull any punches with his words and Tom appreciated him for it. "Tom, is she all right, really?"

"She seems to be handling the situation. Neighbors had already cleared the downed trees in the driveway before we got here and she's been baking up a storm getting stuff ready to take to the shelter tomorrow."

"That's Corin. When there's a disaster, just let her loose in a kitchen."

"She could have worse ways of working off nervous energy."

"Are you making her nervous, Tom?"

"Not trying to."

"Good. Do you think I need to head down there?"

"What did Corin say when you asked?"

"Told me no, flat out."

"Well, I'm learning not to second guess her," Tom teased.

"Smart man that you are, all right, I'll stay here and see what happens. How long will you and your friends stay?"

"We need to head back day after tomorrow. If it dries out a little we'll be able to do some clean up first." There was a resigned sigh and long pause before Bob continued.

"It's too soon, Tom. Give her space."

"If the storm hadn't come in, I wouldn't have come down."

"All right, as long as you're not pushing her."

"Like anyone could push Corin." They shared a laugh over the reality of the statement.

"Tell her to call me tomorrow night to check in, all right?"

"I'll tell her." He hung up the phone but there was no sight of Corin. When she finally returned several minutes later she never mentioned the call or Bob.

Chapter Eight

Later that night, they were relaxing in the family room, the fire burning brightly and the stereo low in the background playing old Miles Davis. They were finishing a second bottle of wine and decided they'd all drive into town tomorrow to see what was happening while Corin dropped off her baked goods. She was at ease with Joe and Anna.

Their conversation took a strange turn earlier in the evening when Corin and Anna were talking about parents. It started out with the twins being away and blossomed into parenting skills and talents. For a while Tom was afraid Anna would ask if she had any children but she hadn't. Instead, they sidetracked to the longevity of marriages. He was smart enough to keep his mouth shut and Joe just listened.

"My parents fought like cats and dogs when we were growing up, but I never felt they were going to divorce, rather it was their way of communicating." Anna said.

"I grew up in Brooklyn with my aunts and uncles living next door or around the corner. We always had family in and out of the house or we were always in theirs. Talk about loud," she laughed. "Try putting eight or ten of us in one room and all trying to get our opinions heard!"

"You make it sound like a battle," Anna teased.

"Sometimes it was. But even then I knew my home would be different. I understood the family wouldn't always be close in location, but I always hoped we'd stay in touch. So far, it's worked. How do

Another Man's Love

you make being on the road work?"

"It's where I want to be. I couldn't have married Joe if I thought he'd leave me home six months of the year. And the girls have adapted. They like their teacher and never would have gotten such intense tutoring as they do one on one. Their reading and math scores are two grades ahead of their age. When we're home for a few months and they're back in their normal school the only thing they want to know is when we're leaving again. We must all have a bit of gypsy blood in us."

"I think it's a great experience for them. The traveling must expose them to so many different places and people." Corin was sitting on the floor with her legs stretched out before her, warming her toes near the fire. Tom was lying on the sofa behind her, holding back the urge to touch her hair or stroke her shoulder. Joe was on the other couch facing them and Anna was curled up against him.

"What about you and Rand, what made you decide to move to the Wilmington area?" Tom tensed but tried not to show it.

"We were in the Hamptons when we met for the second time. He was looking for a place to rent so he could start his next novel. I was out there getting my parents house ready to be put on the market. After the accident, neither Dad nor I spent much time there. It just wasn't the same without Mom. Anyway, after a while we started seeing each other and both knew Manhattan wasn't right for either of us at that point. When we decided to get married, Dad was just retiring to Florida and Rand's mother was already retired there. We got in the car and drove south, looking for a place we both liked." She paused before continuing. "This area felt right. We rented a place for the summer and started looking around. We stumbled onto this place but it was falling down. The estate had let it go to ruin while

101

the heirs fought out who would get it. In the end, they realized the amount of work it needed and were willing to take the cash and run."

"Was it that bad?" Joe asked.

"I have an album full of pictures. It was worse. Poor Rand, he must have thought I'd lost my mind, but he didn't argue. He said if I felt it could be done he'd stick it out. And he did. The first thing we did was have it razed. Of course that meant every ceiling and wall cracked from the lift. Structurally, it needed work anyway. Once razed, the project took on a life of its own. We lived in the apartment over the garage for two years before the county would let us move in."

"I'd love to see those pictures." Corin moved easily from her resting place and took a leather-bound album from a book shelf. Handing it to Anna, she moved back to her place before the fire.

"The staircase had detached from the second floor and there was roof damage, water had been raining in through the attic for a few years. There were termites and just about every other kind of bug you can imagine living here. Birds in the attic and bats in the fireplace, my exterminator and I became fast friends."

Tom shut his eyes and listened to their voices, Corin giving details of the renovation and Anna asking for more particulars. He must have dozed for a while because when he roused Joe was asleep across from him and Anna and Corin were still talking. He lay still with his eyes closed and listened.

"I don't know that we had any real secret to our marriage. I think the only thing we did consistently was not fall out of love at the same time. When one of us was having a moment of anger or depression, the other one was able to take a step back."

"Interesting perspective," Anna noted.

"Well, it allowed us both to be jerks on occasion and know the other one would still be here and vice versa."

"The old, take-a-deep-breath-before-you-speak-kind of thing, I know that one well, with Joe and the girls." They shared a conspiratorial laugh.

"I suppose any good relationship has its version. It worked for Rand and me. But we were both older and wiser, and truly in love. I knew I loved Rand that day in the parking lot when he was all but screaming at me because I dented his precious car. Even then when he was so mad, a part of me saw past his anger. Plus he wasn't hard to look at either." Both women laughed. Tom still didn't let on he was awake.

"We had a better situation than most people. Working from home, we made our own schedule. Rand liked to work from around noon until supper time. We had leisurely mornings together and always the evenings. None of the nine to five pressures. It worked for us. And when one or the other of us felt claustrophobic or cranky, we'd head to neutral corners. I'd go to the studio or Rand would go to his office. We were lucky enough to travel a lot. Rand was always looking for locations for his novels."

"Kind of what Joe and I have; only there are always more people around us."

"Rand used to kid that we were in a perpetual state of hotel sex. Since we didn't live on a time schedule it was like always being on vacation. We were relaxed and tuned into each other, mentally and physically."

"Yes, I can relate to that," Anna said. Their conversation turned back to traveling and being away from home for so long.

****

Tom wondered what Corin would do if she

traveled with him. Would she paint? What would she do without a kitchen to work in when she was restless? Would she be content in his lifestyle? The possibilities were overwhelming when he put them into that perspective.

He let his mind wander to his marriages. There was never that give and take in either of them. He realized early on before he met either one of them his music came first and that meant he came first. Rarely had he been the one to take a step back. His ex-wives considered him hard and cold. In truth, he just didn't care enough to work on the relationships.

When Joe met Anna their relationship changed the way Joe looked at life. He too had been guilty of putting the music first, until he met Anna. Then she came first and while Tom understood it, he couldn't see it happening for him. When they were expecting the girls and Amber started talking about babies, he'd gone on the defensive and put himself first.

That was when he knew it was himself, not the music first. Since then he'd all but shut down inside. Women were occasional and always plentiful if he was interested. In the last few years he hadn't been interested. Two or three dates was enough for him, most often ending the relationship before it could turn into one.

Then on a rainy weekend in February, life as he knew it changed. Tom had acknowledged and tolerated the changes because he had no choice. But finding out Rand had died was like fate giving him one last chance at a life he'd never thought to have for himself. For the first time since the operation he started to think his vasectomy could be reversed. The idea of a child or two wasn't daunting as it once seemed, as long as Corin was their mother. Nothing else would be acceptable. Here he was, in her home again and he'd managed to annoy and alienate her with just about every breath.

****

Tom woke from the nightmare in a sweat, his body tangled in the down comforter. He knew immediately where he was even in the dark, knew she was all right but he didn't try to go back to sleep. Afraid the image would return he scrubbed his hands across his face and pulled on jeans before heading downstairs. While there was no loud noise, diffused light told him she was up and moving around in the kitchen. Watching her from the doorway she had no idea she wasn't alone. Even Beau didn't announce his arrival; after taking a look, the dog simply dropped his head back to the floor.

Corin stood forming something into ball-shapes, then flatting them slightly before placing them on a tray. His stomach churned at the sight of her bruised shoulder and knew it would get worse before it got better. It wasn't until she turned and pushed the faucet on that his reflection in the window over the sink startled her, she let out a quick screeching sound. Her sticky fingers flew to her throat, as they did, small bits of the mixture stuck to her skin.

"I'm sorry, I didn't mean to scare you," he started.

"Jeez, Tom, you took ten years off me that time." Turning quickly, she moved her hands under the running water, washing away the remnants of debris. "Can't sleep?" she finally managed to ask.

"I did for a while, I had a dream...," he started and didn't finish. He saw her studying him from the reflection. He wondered what he saw but didn't ask.

"That bad?" Corin turned with the dish towel in her hand watching him openly. "Want to talk about it?" Using the edge of the cloth she wiped the mixture from her chest.

"I don't think you want to hear." He moved to a cabinet and pulled down a glass before going to the water dispenser in the refrigerator door. The cold liquid woke up his insides and forced the cobwebs from his brain. "What are you doing up? It's only four o'clock."

"I couldn't sleep, figured I get a jump on things for tomorrow or today, whichever."

"Corin?"

"I sleep, Tom, just in short spurts. Besides, the crab cakes need to be frozen for a while. They'll fry up better tonight and the flavors will have a chance to meld."

"I thought we were taking you out tonight?" She only smiled and turned away with the tray in her hand.

"I have a freezer full of meat, remember?"

"Still?" His fingers brushed back a stray lock of his hair and Corin again watched the movement of his hand until she realized he was watching her watch him. She laughed outright at him.

"Do you have any idea what was in that crate you sent us?" Still standing across the room to keep his distance he only let one shoulder raise. "It was almost a whole side of beef," she told him good naturedly. "Rand and I had several meals, and I've fed not only Bob but my dad several times while he was here and there's still steaks left. So tonight, we'll throw them on the grill and have a quick relaxing meal."

"And that's why you're making...what are you making?"

"Crab cakes."

"And you always make crab cakes at four in the morning."

"No, only when my mind is preoccupied." Her look dared him to ask but he didn't. "Tell me about your dream, Tom."

Corin quickly cleaned the counters and pulled a carton of orange juice from the refrigerator. Filling two glasses she set one in front of him and moved to an end drawer. He watched her pull a pack of cigarettes and lighter from it before turning. "On the porch, all right? I don't smoke in the house." She didn't wait to see if he followed, assuming he would eventually.

"I didn't know you smoked," he said when they were finally settled on the back porch, a light throw pulled across her almost bare shoulders. Corin wore a pair of thin cotton pants and a matching cotton camisole. Her feet were bare as usual, tucked up under her in the old wicker rocker.

"Only occasionally and usually with Bob, he's a bad influence."

"Yeah, why now?"

"Because I wanted one since the storm hit and didn't. Now I just want it, I feel like I earned it." He didn't try and argue the point further.

"Tell me about the dream."

"I dreamt you were falling from the roof and when I tried to catch you I missed." He surprised himself with the bluntness of his words.

"Well, talk about your subconscious mind taking over," she teased, trying to defuse his anger.

"Damn it, Corin, you could have been seriously hurt. As it is you are hurt."

"It's just a couple of scratches, Tom, nothing more than when I'd scrape my knee when I was a kid."

"We're not kids Corin, and it could have been worse. What if you had fallen and there was nobody around to help you?" He held her look, daring her to turn away.

"Don't go there, all right? You make me sound like some old fart who should be wearing a monitor around my neck." She drew on the cigarette and seemed instantly calmed by the motion. "I visited that place myself today and I didn't like it. I had my cell phone in my pocket!" She rolled her eyes at him as if to imply she wasn't completely stupid.

"Well at least you have some sense left!"

"You know, ever since you got here you've been treating me like a child who isn't taking your orders. I'm an adult woman Tom and like it or not I will make my own decisions and live with the consequences." Her voice rose and her eyes narrowed.

Even in the dim light he knew he'd riled her up once again. The tip of her cigarette glowed as she drew against the tobacco tube. Tom slipped it from her fingers, taking one than another deep drag from it, savoring the taste and experiencing the slight rush before handing it back.

"I know you're not a child, Corin. If you were I wouldn't be in the position I'm in."

"And what position is that?"

"The position that puts me head over heels in love with a woman who still loves her dead husband." His words stung them both but he didn't apologize. "I can't compete with a ghost."

****

She wasn't sure if he was telling her or himself. He simply left the seat beside her and went back inside. Corin didn't follow him; she stayed where she was, watching the sun rise while she tried to force thoughts of them together from her mind. She'd wanted to kiss him, to explore him, learning his taste and scent. Instead she'd sent him away with angry words when she realized how attracted she was to him.

It was hard not to be, considering he was still tousled from sleep. His blonde hair in complete disarray, his hazel eyes dreamy and he was shirtless. She didn't stop the open appraisal of his broad shoulders and chest, the light mat of curling hairs disappearing under the waist band of his jeans. His stomach flat and firm and her fingers wanted to dance across his abs. She wondered if he was ticklish or not and forced herself not to think of him.

When she saw him several hours later it was simple to ignore their early morning encounter. She acted as if nothing had happened between them, handing him a mug of coffee when he entered the kitchen. Bacon was frying and she was grilling thick slabs of French toast.

"Morning," she started as he took several long sips. Glancing around he noted they were alone.

"Anyone else up?" he asked.

"Anna and Joe are out for a walk. They went down to the end of the driveway to get the newspaper."

"How long ago?"

"They just left," she answered automatically. She flipped the toast slices and was about to move away when he blocked her path. He put the mug aside, his hand reaching to her chin. Tom's fingers held her lightly where he wanted her as his mouth descended.

****

Corin watched him wide-eyed for several seconds before skin touched skin. She braced herself for a punishing kiss but got soft and seductive instead. He didn't plunder into her mouth, rather tasted and explored her with an erotic edge. Only when she sighed and leaned towards him did he deepen his assault. His tongue teased her bottom lip then her top before venturing to meet hers. Corin dropped the kitchen towel she held and let herself rise to meet him.

Tom pulled back slightly and studied her face before leaning back in for a second kiss. This time Corin's hands rose to his shoulders and explored the warm strength he presented. With just a hint of cooperation from her, he pulled her against his chest and took the kiss she'd begun to wonder about; Tom pulled back when he became fully aroused and he repositioned her between his legs against it. He took a step back and leaned on the counter.

"Damn it, Corin," he started and she laughed. He wasn't happy about her laughing but he knew it was a defense. With a muttered curse he turned away. "We've got to get out of this house," he said more to himself than to her.

"Yes," was all she said before remembering the food on the grill. She managed to get to it just before it would have burned. By the time they both recovered from the strength of the kiss, Anna and Joe arrived back with the paper. There was only a slight skirmish over whose vehicle they would use and who would drive it. Corin's rationalization about gasoline availability and her knowledge of the area back roads had them finally loaded into her SUV with her driving. Anna rode shotgun and the two men in the back seat were still stunned they weren't in control.

Tom watched her pack several small cartons with ready made meals in Styrofoam containers, his mouth watering at the scent of grilled chicken and the honey ham she sliced. Conversation centered on food that didn't need refrigeration and the lack of mayonnaise use. Each container held either a chicken meal complete with biscuits and collards or ham with green beans and potato salad made with a mustard dressing. Several pieces of fruit were layered and then a cinnamon roll and blueberry muffin. She'd even tucked in some napkins.

Joe had watched the process from the counter, impressed at the assembly line process. He and Tom had tasted slices of the ham and were promised their own lunch after their journey. Even on full stomachs from their recent breakfast the two men were already looking forward to lunch.

The back of Corin's SUV was carefully arranged. She'd done it of course, Tom instinctively knew better than to offer suggestions. Not being able to find fault with her process nagged at him a bit as they slowly navigated the rutted driveway her eyes glancing to the rear view mirror to see his slight pout.

Their first stop was Mrs. Larsen's place. She lived up the road from Corin and just as far back. Her home was a one level ranch that sat on an open acre and ran straight to the ocean. Corin met her on the porch, introducing her friends and inquiring about storm damage. Tom nodded, remembering her from the Sunday supper. From his position in the driveway his mind was more on the ocean view than the words passing between them. Corin watched as he and Joe wandered towards the water line. From his last visit, he was able to give Joe a quick lesson on retaining walls and piers with docks.

Their second stop was in the other direction and on the other side of the road. The elderly man who lived in the small saltbox home with its weathered wood siding and metal roof relied heavily on his cane. Corin again introduced her friends but the wooded lot didn't garner his attention. He listened to their conversation openly.

"You know how these Yankees are, they hardly eat enough to fill a mouse."

"You're one to be talking, missy, you're one of them too," he said back with a wink.

The discussion went from storm damage to when power would come back. Corin had slipped into his home with the carton and returned quickly to the porch. Mr. Walters was inviting them in for a glass of tea but Corin refused, reminding him of the rest of the deliveries she needed make. She offered to take him into town to see what was going on but he declined. After bringing two plastic gallon jugs of water to the porch she asked if he'd been taking his medicine. Assured he was, they went on their way.

As they neared the center of town storm damage increased. Trees and limbs were pushed off to the sides of the road and the road itself was tricky in places. As they drove it wasn't uncommon to see a tree leaning on a roof or engulfing a stray vehicle. Power company trucks from several surrounding areas were hard at work. Nearing the center of the small beach town the ruin worsened. One street would look virtually untouched while the next one had taken a hit. It was an extremely sobering drive.

Corin parked on a side street and they all walked down to the far corner where it had been roped off because of high water. She saw several people and the short conversations were the same, "How bad did you get hit and it could have been worse."

For some of the residents, it was worse. Some homes wouldn't be lived in again or at least for a long time. The commercial section of town took minimal water and wind. Corin wove her way through the people with definite purpose. When she stopped beside the pharmacy, the man in the doorway asked the same question, "How bad?"

Corin's last stop was the school that had been set up as a temporary shelter. It took two trips to empty her truck and she introduced her company to all.

****

The school was relatively new, housing grades K through twelve in three separate wings that shared common gyms and auditorium. It was easy to wander away, walking the cool dark halls and glancing in classrooms. It brought back memories he'd not let himself think of for years. Corin found him studying a bulletin board, the schedules and lunch room menus catching his eye. She wondered what childhood memory surfaced for Tom entering the building.

She studied him the entire time she'd been walking towards him. Corin saw only Tom Hayden and let herself get excited about the tingling in her belly when she did. He was tall and lean but not thin. His shoulders and chest were well defined as was his flat stomach. His legs were long; his thighs muscled under the denim. His blonde hair was long enough to brush his collar and she now knew how the texture of his skin felt under her touch. Warmth rushed through her and she savored the long lost feeling. Moving quietly beside him she waited for him to acknowledge her.

"I can't remember the last time I was in a school, probably graduation," Tom said, acknowledging her.

"It has its own feel and smell, doesn't it? Like a locker room with over currents of crayons and chalk."

"The first girl I ever kissed was in second grade, on the playground." He shifted his weight to his left hip.

"Started young," Corin said. "Do you remember her name and did she like the kiss?"

Tom turned and smiled. "Her name was Pam Gilson and she was a brunette too." He let his hand rise, his fingers sifting Corin's short curls. "And I guess she didn't like it because we never kissed again."

His fingers threaded against her scalp, cupping her head to the angle he wanted. She didn't stop him, didn't resist. She let her mouth drop open, an invitation to his action.

"I'm sure you've practiced since then." Corin was surprised at the husky tone of her own words, muddled because she wanted his touch, his kiss.

"Try me, Corin," Tom whispered just before he

took her lips under his. Neither of them cared that they were in a public place and anyone could turn the corner and find them. They took it as a moment in time where nothing else mattered. Warm and tender quickly turned intense, Corin leaned into him, making her own demands on his mouth. Her hand moved over his chest, his heart beating rapidly under her palm.

She forgot to breathe, forgot how until he pulled away. His forehead dropped to hers until their breathing calmed, his fingers didn't untangle from her hair. They heard voices in the distance and he begrudgingly let her go. Composed somewhat by the time he was introduced to the school principal, it turned into a long, quiet ride home.

***

Corin spent most of the ride absorbing what she'd learned about Tom Hayden during their trip. She'd studied his expressions in the rear view mirror when they came to a particularly hard hit area. She'd watched and listened to him interact with some of the people they met. It left her with an oddly displaced feeling by the time they made it back to her house for lunch. A part of her wanted to be able to dismiss him, yet that hadn't happened. He'd been sympathetic towards anyone whom had damage and listened patiently to their tale of storms and angst. She'd assumed he'd be terse and edgy but in reality he'd been sensitive towards their fears.

As promised, they lunched on thick slices of ham and potato salad and all wound up on the front porch afterwards. Joe and Anna were on the swing and Corin and Tom settled into large chairs, a small table separating them. Conversation was put aside for the newspaper and Anna's book. Corin closed her eyes and woke with a start only minutes later, refreshed and only slightly embarrassed. After minimal discussion, Anna went with her to the

114

studio, the men stayed behind to finish the paper.

****

Supper turned into an evening event. They'd devoured her crab cakes and the steaks they'd grilled. Nearing nine that night the power flickered several times. Corin waited until the back-up system shut down and the current ran continuously before she got up to re-set the blinking clocks. They'd spent the rest of the evening in the family room before the fire, the lights turned down low in similar positions to the night before.

Joe told Corin about the trouble Tom's infamous truck had given him and Corin laughed openly. Realizing it was the first time she'd laughed all weekend gave Tom an unsettled feeling. The conversation turned to her SUV and the safety factors that made it her choice. Tom was surprised as the words came from her easily.

"Ten years ago I was in an accident. My mom was driving and didn't survive. After that I had to make a decision. I could never get in another vehicle ever again but that didn't seem too realistic, so I decided if I had to drive, it would be in what made me feel safe."

"It must have been nerve-wracking to drive the first time after something like that?" Anna put in. "I've only had a few fender benders, thank God, nothing like what you experienced and ask Joe, it took a long time for me to drive after each one."

"The first time wasn't hard after I made the decision. I had Ted, my ex-husband, take me to a mall parking lot late one night. I drove around it for a long time before I drove us home. It was getting on the same stretch of road where the accident happened that always made me queasy."

"What about when you hit Rand's Jaguar?" Tom inserted.

"That was nothing, didn't even dent my rear

bumper." She said it with a straight face before smiling. "Now his car, well, it needed work!"

"I never would have met you if it hadn't been for my truck."

"I know, and at times you must think it was a mixed blessing." Tom stared for several seconds before laughing. After that, it was easy to change the subject with the request of coffee.

Chapter Nine

Corin stood in the darkened doorway to her living room listening to the notes Tom Hayden played on the piano. For a long time neither of them said anything and she wasn't sure if he knew she was there.

"It's beautiful, is it from the new album?"

"No," he answered a bit too quickly. She moved into the room aware of his maleness. He wore only jeans, was shirtless and barefoot, sitting in her living room and she wanted to throw him to the floor and have her way with him. Instead, she put the instrument between them, afraid what might happen if she sat beside him on the bench.

"It's almost seductive," she started, than asked, "What's it called?"

"You don't want to know," Tom told her.

"As in that's the title or it's none of my business?"

"Be careful what questions you ask, Corin, you might not like the answers."

"Oh," was all she managed.

During a prolonged silence, he kept playing the piece, over and over, as if taunting her to ask again. Instead, he asked her what he wanted to know. Somehow in the dead of night it seemed right. Corin knew they'd probably not be alone again before they left tomorrow.

"You should be sleeping," he said off-handedly.

"So should you, you've got a long drive ahead of you tomorrow."

"We'll be all right; there are three of us to do the

117

driving."

"You mean you'd actually let Anna drive. Your ego would survive?"

"You drove today and I managed to get through it."

"But just barely!" He accepted her answer and didn't argue. That was when she knew she was right. And she understood she'd love this man differently from any other in her past. A warming thought came with the acceptance of her realization.

"I'm willing to share some of the burden, Corin. I can accept help when I need it."

"Are you saying I can't?"

"I'm saying you've got a lot of responsibility on your shoulders right now and nobody to share it with. And you seem unwilling to let me help."

"Right now, there's nothing that can really be done. Believe it or not, your visit was the best thing for me."

"Sure, three more people to cook for," he said.

"That too, you were a diversion and trust me, I needed one badly right now." Corin let her mind clear and listened to the music he played. She'd never forget the melody, somehow she knew it was important but couldn't get a grip on why.

When he spoke she broke herself away from the thoughts forming in the back of her mind. The act would be so simple, all she had to do was walk towards him, her hand raised and she'd have contact with him, with his bare skin against her touch. Thankful it was dark; she hoped he hadn't seen her cheeks heat.

"Tell me about the accident, Corin," he said, his voice steady.

"What does it matter anymore?"

He stopped playing and looked directly at her. "Because it's shaped you into the woman you've become."

"I suppose you're right," she said hesitantly, acknowledging his importance in her life, before taking a deep breath. Tom watched her sort it out in her mind, what and how she would tell him.

"It was the beginning of April, the first Thursday, Mom and I were driving out east. We were going to open up the house in the Hamptons, get some groceries, generally just air it out and Dad and Ted were supposed to take the train out the following evening. We'd just passed through Riverhead and were debating what to do first when it started raining."

She couldn't avoid visualizing the stretch of road as she talked about it.

"It was just a light sprinkle, a cloudburst really; you could still see the sun shining in the distance. Late in the afternoon, we were both happy to be heading to the beach and grumbling about the work ahead." Corin realized her hands had gone to her belly, stroking it as she had when she was pregnant, then paused and moved closer to the front window, her hands warming her upper arms, her back to him now.

"It didn't really rain, just drizzled enough to make the road slick. We didn't see him until he was directly in front of us." She took a deep breath preparing herself. "The deer came out of nowhere. Mom swerved to miss him and hit a skid. She tried to correct it but we went off the side of the road and flipped. Eventually we wound up in a thicket of trees."

Tom didn't prompt her, somehow knowing she'd tell him in her own time.

"I remember waking up and being pinned. Later I found out I'd broken my left leg and hip, crushed my pelvis and collapsed a lung along with various other bumps and bruises. Sometimes I wonder what might have been different if we'd had cell phones back than." She hesitated then visibly shook off the sadness. "I don't know how long I was unconscious. I tried to wake Mom and couldn't. It was raining harder and..." Corin stopped then went back to the piano, pulling the picture of her parents towards her, studying it as if she'd never see it before, wondering what Tom would see when he looked at it.

"Nobody found us for a long time," she finally finished.

"Corin, I'm sorry."

"So was I. For all the things I never told her and all the time we never got to spend together. For the child neither of us ever got to hold." She put the picture back and moved beside him on the bench. "This was hers. It was her prized possession. When I was a kid she wanted me to take lessons but I just didn't get it. Music I mean, the notes...It was like a foreign language to me. I promised myself one day I'd learn but I still haven't. You're the first person to play it, in years."

"Does that bother you?"

"That you're playing it, no. Only that it's a beautiful instrument and never gets used."

"Rand didn't play?" Corin laughed openly beside him. "I'm tone deaf and can't carry a tune. Rand was worse. His hearing was shot on his left side. Something from the service, he never really elaborated, only as he aged he was losing hearing in that side." Corin stopped and looked at Tom, deciding how much to tell him. "Actually, at times it was a Godsend, when I wanted to snip at him I could, if I was on the correct side." She laughed and so did Tom.

"Of course he knew about it?"

"Of course, it wouldn't have been any fun if he hadn't."

"You're a hard woman, Corin."

"Sometimes yes, other times difficult as you've

undoubtedly found out." He went back to the melody and played it continuously.

"Finish telling me Corin, and I promise I'll never ask again." She wanted to snuggle against his bare chest but didn't.

"Dad got worried when he tried to call later that night. He was the one who called the police and begged them to look for the car. They told him no accidents had been reported involving Mom's car or our names. He was upset and eventually talked them into checking our route. I don't know what time they finally found us, it was well into the night. Raining harder than I think I've ever seen it rain. It took them over an hour to get us out. Mom was long gone by then and I knew, I just knew my baby was gone too, I knew I'd been bleeding...there wasn't anything I could do pinned under the dashboard."

She stood abruptly and went back to the window. "I was into the fifth month and I knew deep inside the baby wasn't going to survive and at that point I didn't want to either. After they got me out I don't remember much, only pain. Bob was there when I woke up and my dad. Nine days had passed; I'd missed Mom's and the baby's funeral. They buried them together."

Corin left abruptly but came back shortly with several tissues in her hand finishing without prompting. "Anyway, I'm not sure what I remember of those first nine days, some time's I think the memories are from those first days waking and sometimes I think they were while I was semiconscious. Either way, it didn't matter. I'd had to have major surgery for internal injuries. And they told me then I probably would have trouble conceiving again, when I tried. They'd done the best they could, putting me back together, but it was an unknown about my carrying to term if I could conceive. After that, it was all a blur, a month in the hospital and then in a nursing home before I was strong enough to spend months at a rehab facility. They had to teach me to walk again and I had no strength at all. It was just short of six months before I finally went home. I had a cane for the rest of that first year until my balance finally clicked back into place."

"Six months," he hissed, stunned at the notion of what she must have gone through to recover so fully.

"Six months. I probably could have gone home sooner but Ted wanted me to be one hundred percent. As time went on I understood why, he was pulling away from me. I was damaged and so was our dream. We wouldn't have the family we always talked about. We'd never be the same people again. Oh, he tried; at least I thought he was at the time. The first weeks I was home he was all over me, any want or whims just ask. I suppose I should have leaned on him more, but I felt I had to do everything myself or I might never do it again. My therapist was wonderful. She put all my guilt into perspective plus my drive to make everything perfect around me. Only it wasn't perfect anymore. That was when I did the first self-portrait. My husband didn't want a damaged woman on his hands and I couldn't forgive him for that. If he loved me as much as he always said he did, it shouldn't have mattered. But in the end it did."

Corin hesitated and decided to tell him the rest truthfully. "He'd been having an affair before I got pregnant and he continued it while I was recuperating. That was one of his reasons for me being one hundred percent before coming home; it bought him more time with her. I always wondered if he'd been the one to get careless with her things in our apartment but came to realize they both did. The first time I found underwear that wasn't mine he made me think I was crazy, that it was mine and I'd just forgotten. But she'd left other hints only a woman would understand."

"Like what?" His voice was barely recognizable.

"A different brand of tampon discreetly stowed in my bathroom. Make up that was the wrong shade for me and ultimately I found some jewelry that was never mine. She'd left a trendy initial bracelet with a prominent 'R' in our bedroom. He had the balls to tell me one day that, 'A man needs his outlets!' That was the day I knew the marriage was over. I moved back to Brooklyn with Dad and later found out he'd gotten his girlfriend pregnant. From that moment on our divorce was a breeze."

"Anything else?" Tom said

"Bob was wonderful. If it hadn't been for him those first months in rehab I don't know how far I might have come. He bullied and chastised and pushed all the right buttons to get me up and out of the wheelchair. He stuck by me during the separation and the divorce." She hesitated but finally finished. "He'd known or at least suspected about Ted's affair. He couldn't believe how little time Ted actually spent with me in the hospital. Bob got friendly with the nurses and they were the ones who told him of Ted's exaggerated stories of staying by my side when nobody else was around. Apparently he'd taken to showing up just before he knew the rest of the family would and after they left, he'd slip away. But I've got to give him credit; he never said an ill word against Ted until I moved back to Brooklyn with Dad. That was when he finally let me know what had really been going on. My father had known too, although I don't think Bob was the one to tell him. He'd known from the start that Ted's actions were all for show. Apparently he was less guarded at the wake and made some comments about having lost a son. That's what I can't forgive him for. My mother was gone and so was our child

123

and he'd been upset because it was a boy. If it had been a girl he wouldn't have cared."

"Your husband was an idiot, Corin."

"Hindsight and all that, yes I agree. I sometimes wonder what would have happened if we hadn't had the accident. What would I have done when I found out about his affair? What lengths I'd have gone to, to keep us together for the baby. He once told me in a fit of anger that he could have forgiven mom if I'd been carrying a girl, but since it was a boy he'd never forgive her or me completely. I couldn't stop myself from wondering what I'd done wrong to make him feel he needed another woman, even before I found out I was pregnant. I never realized..."

"And Bob let this man live? I guess I gave him too much credit."

"He didn't want to," Corin said with a smile. "But I made him see he'd created his own hell with his new wife and child. We ran into them a few years later, Rand and I were in Manhattan with Bob at Christmas time. We were all at Rockefeller Center watching the skaters and there they were. The whole family unit, Ted, Regina and their perfect first born son and their daughter. But the kids were loud and obnoxious. Poetic justice if you ask me. His perfect ideal was exactly what he'd wanted and gotten and he still wasn't happy. Regina didn't look very happy either."

"Good, you're right, poetic justice."

"There's more," she said with a conspiratorial laugh, lightening the moment. "He called me a few days later and asked to see me, for old time's sake."

Tom stopped playing. "You've got to be kidding?"

"No, he had a brass set. He told me I looked wonderful and we should get together to reminisce. Reminisce my ass, he wanted one last lay."

"What did you tell him?"

"I gave the phone to Rand and let him tell Ted

what he thought of the idea."

Tom threw back his head laughing, not needing to know the exact words Rand might have used. Knowing what he would have said in the same situation was enough.

"When did you start painting?"

"Right after I got out of the rehab center. I wasn't much for leaving home in those first months. It was a good way to express frustration and bitterness. After I moved back to Brooklyn it seemed a reasonable way to work out my hostility about Ted's extracurricular activities."

"I wish I'd bought those paintings when I'd seen them."

"I'm glad you didn't. They were very dark and moody, quite depressive as I remember. Letting them go was very therapeutic from a strange perspective."

"But suited to my mood sometimes."

"So now you know, did I leave anything out, anything you're not clear about?"

"Yes. You said you would have trouble conceiving, you never wanted to try?"

"No. I thought about it a lot after the divorce, I did some research on clinical ways to go about it with a donor. But that was right around the time I met Rand. He let me know up front, before he knew the particulars about my situation he'd had a vasectomy years earlier and he didn't want children. Oddly enough, when I really sat down and thought it through, being with Rand was what I truly wanted, and it took the pressure off me. There would be no waiting each month to find out and no despair that would come with each period. I suppose the true unknown was even if I could conceive could I carry to term? With Rand I knew it would be him and me. That was enough. He made me very happy. For the first time since the accident I was truly content with my situation. I guess because it wasn't relevant anymore. Instead, we traveled and we found this place. By then I was ready for a project and as this got closer to being finished, he kept prompting me to start painting again."

"And if he hadn't passed away, you'd still be happy here with him."

"Yes, I like to think so. But that's not a reality anymore. Now I have to find out what is."

"Well, do me a favor when you're thinking about it," he stopped to watch her closely. She nodded he should continue. "Think about what it might be like to have me in your life. I know it would be drastically different, Corin. I live in Boston and I tour six months sometimes more. But it's a good life if you have the right person beside you."

"Like Joe and Anna?"

"Yes, but we're different people and we'd be different."

"All right, I'll think about it."

"Good, there's just one other thing you have a right to know." He continued with a resigned sigh. "Years ago, my second wife Amber wanted to start a family. I didn't. Not with her. I had a vasectomy too."

"What did she think about that?"

"I never told her. When she wasn't getting pregnant and I wasn't sharing her frustration over it, she moved on to someone more sympathetic."

"You never told her?" Corin couldn't believe what she was hearing.

"No. Actually, you're one of the few people who know. Even Joe and Anna don't know I had it done. It wasn't their business. All I knew was that I didn't want to bring children into this world with Amber as their mother." He added, "I never really trusted her and I never opened myself up to her completely. Not the way we talk, Corin, here or on the phone. What ever we decide this relationship is, it's the most honest I've ever had. I appreciate it and abhor it at the same time. You make me vulnerable; it's not a comfortable place to be."

"Oh," she managed.

"I'm trying to be as honest as I can Corin, right from the start with you." Their talk turned the mood around them heavy. She was the one who leaned towards him and touched her lips lightly to his.

"Thank you for telling me. I understand our relationship is...different. I knew it the last time you were here only wouldn't admit it to myself. For the first time since I'd run into Rand in the Hamptons, I looked at a man, you, and I saw you as male, not just a man."

She remembered watching him sleep on her porch. "That afternoon in the studio, I still don't know why I showed you the nudes. I didn't rationalize it, only that it felt right. I didn't stop to think of the implications at the time, just that it seemed natural. I told myself it was because I saw you as an artist who works in a different medium, that you'd get the premise. But since our phone calls started I've had to accept that there was more behind it I refused to see."

"This song, this melody, you're the only other person to hear it. We talked about some things that weren't for public consumption; this is one of them, for now. It's still too personal to me."

"Why?"

"Because it's not mine anymore, it's yours. And until I know where we're going I can't let go of the song. If you decide you don't want me around, it's all I'll have left of you."

They were both quiet for too long, Corin finally rousing herself from visions of lying with him. "I have one question?"

"Go ahead."

"What's the title to the song you're playing?"

"Another Man's Love," he told her with no hesitation.

"Oh," was all she managed. He burst out laughing reminding her she shouldn't ask if she didn't want to know.

"Are there any lyrics?"

"Yes." He lowered his voice and quietly sang the first lines.

"We were never supposed to meet, but fate called our bluff. She's everything I ever wanted, but dared not dream. She's another man's love, she doesn't notice me. She's another man's wife, she'll never be free."

Corin didn't say a word when he finished, she just turned into his waiting arms and let her tears fall against his naked chest. When she'd composed herself she managed to pull back and look at him.

"I asked...," she said with a smile and didn't pull away from his kisses. Different from the others they'd shared this day, this one sensual and erotic. As if he understood her need and tried to sooth her. When he finally pulled away she slipped from the bench beside him and moved towards the stairway. She turned and spoke quietly before leaving him alone in the dark room.

"Thank you for telling me, Tom. Keep me posted with your progress on the new album. I hope you can get some sleep." Corin forced herself to walk away, to take each step one at a time and lock herself away behind her bedroom door, because at this time in her life, she wanted Tom Hayden. Beyond the physical she wanted him for herself and the idea scared the hell out of her.

Chapter Ten

Sleep was the last thing on his mind at the moment and he knew better than to try. He played the melody over and over, new lyrics forming in the back of his mind. The original depressive ballad was taking a different turn.

Waking slowly, her voice was part of the dream, her words whisper soft, "Tommy, come with me," she repeated several times. His body moved into a languid stretch before he opened his eyes and found her kneeling beside the sofa he'd stretched out on. After their conversation at the piano last night he hadn't bothered to go back to bed, when his eyes blurred he dropped on the sofa. He had no idea what time it was only dark still. "Tommy, come with me," she said again, this time her slim fingers were reaching towards him.

Contact with his chest made him draw a breath, her touch a mere fluttering.

"Corin?" Her touch made him realize the voice wasn't part of his dream.

"Come with me," she repeated as she stood and waited for him to do the same. He reached for the hand she held out towards him and followed her. When they neared the second floor landing he thought she'd take him into his guest room, but instead she tugged him further towards another door at the far end of the hallway. It opened quietly before a long, narrow staircase. At the top landing Tom hesitated, taking in the space around him.

Obviously the attic, it was set up as a game room of sorts. The back wall was anchored with three large double hung windows looking out to the ocean. Under it was a thickly padded window seat with several throw pillows tossed about. Across from the window was a full sofa upholstered in a spring plaid. Two solid colored club chairs flanked it with plaid pillows. There was a large square wood coffee table in the center, a coordinating area rug pulling the whole place together.

To one side was a set of bunk beds and across the room were two twin beds. Built in bookcases housed games and magazines, a television and stereo. Tom took his time exploring the space. One wall shelf held the complete Nancy Drew mystery series and below it the Hardy Boys. There were stacks of old video tapes from Disney movies to Star Wars. Behind the sofa was an old foosball table.

"What is this space, Corin?" She'd gone directly to the window and huddled into the corner of the bench seat, pulling a pillow onto her lap, her fingers tugging at the fringe.

Awake now, he studied her in the distance, the non existent lighting no help. She'd changed into soft looking yellow sweat pants and a matched front zippered sweat top. She had thick cotton socks on her feet and her face was washed clean, her hair brushed from her face.

"A rec room of sorts, a few extra beds, a place to hang out on a rainy day when I get hormonal or depressed."

"Are you depressed now, Corin?" She didn't look up at him only shook her head.

"No, I'm confused Tom. Rand never spent much time up here; I didn't know where else to bring you, he's all around the house and the property. I wanted to talk to you and I know in the morning there won't be time."

"Talk about what?" He moved slowly through the space and sat heavily on the center of the sofa, directly across from her.

"About you, Tom, about some of the things you said this weekend."

"Pick one." While the two words came out as a dare she decided he hadn't meant to be combative. He settled back and propped his feet on the table in front of him, waiting for her to start. After all, she'd brought him up here, he'd let her have her say.

"Start with, you're head over heels in love with a woman who loves her dead husband and you can't compete with a ghost."

"I was being honest, completely. And when you get to know me better you'll come to realize just how hard that is for me sometimes. It's much easier not to let anyone near than to be disappointed by them. Especially in my business, everyone wants something from me, Corin. I've learned to deflect outsiders. But you, you got me on a gut level the first time I saw you."

He dropped his feet and leaned forward, his elbows propped on his thighs, his hands holding his head. "Damn it, Corin," he said, shaking his head as he settled back. "You came bustling down the hall in some silky black slip of a thing pulling on Rand's shirt, your hair mussed and your lips full and just short of being bruised. You had the look of a woman who was being thoroughly ravished when we interrupted. And everything aside, I saw the recognition on your face when you realized it was Bob. It was like you lit up from the inside. At that very second I wanted you to react to me that same way. The next second I looked at your very protective husband and knew it would never happen." Tom stood and walked around the space before continuing. "That's when the first lines of the song came to me. The notes just fell into place. Sometimes it just happens that way. The words and music just gel inside me."

"You don't really know me, how could you think you love me?"

"I didn't say it made sense, just that it was how I felt."

"I don't know how to react to you Tom. There's a side of me that wants to explore you. You, the man who is so close just now, bare-chested and bold. A side of me wants to jump you, plain and simple, to experience you as a man. And there's a part of me that feels like it would be cheating on Rand, even though that's ridiculous. Can you really cheat on a dead person?" She drew a breath and let it out slowly. "And there's a portion of me that wants to believe a man like you could actually have feelings for me. But that's the part I just don't get, why me? You must come in contact with so many women, besides the fans throwing themselves at you, why me? Is it because I was married and you couldn't have me or something else? Do you consider me your muse for the song? What happens when you finish it, would you still want me then? And what would happen if I called your bluff and told you to take me right here, right now?" Of all the points she'd mentioned he homed in on the last one.

"Not here, Corin. Not in his home."

"It's my home too."

"It's your home with him. There's a difference."

"Like it would be cheating to make love to me in his home?"

"Something like that."

"All right, we agree this isn't the place. But what happens now, Tom? What do you really want to happen? In a few hours you'll pack your rented truck and head back north and get on with the tour. What do you expect to happen then?"

"I don't know Corin. I hadn't really thought it through. Only that I needed you to understand I can't get you out of my mind, no matter how hard I try. Most of all I wanted you to know you weren't alone. That you could call me and I'd do just about anything in my power to make you happy. Crazy isn't it? You pissed me off big time when you wouldn't leave here during the storm; I wanted to wring some sense into you..." Corin watched as his hands tightened into fists and relaxed.

"I get that from a lot of people," she teased, lightening his darkening mood.

"Yeah, I can relate. But the thing is I understand why you didn't leave, even though I didn't agree. When I thought it through, remembered how much time and energy you put into the old place I could understand it, to a degree. But Corin, it's still just a structure. If something had happened to you, I don't know what I'd have done. And ultimately that's why I rented the truck and drove down here two days ago. I had to know for myself that not only were you intact, but that the house was still here for you."

"It seems I've been causing you a lot of trouble since we met."

"I saw the way you loved your husband, Corin. I've never been loved like that. I wanted you to love me with the same intensity and trust."

"If we had any kind of a relationship it would be different. What's between us already is on many levels."

"I agree, but I know the woman you are inside, Corin. You're strong and determined yet kind and loving. You're funny and protective. I wanted you to see me as special."

"The problem is to a certain degree I do, Tom and being honest, it scares the hell out of me. I'm a housewife from North Carolina, not the kind of woman who meets and falls in love with a rock and roll icon and has her feelings returned. You're supposed to be with some super model or exotic talented beautiful woman. Not me."

"I can't help that I fell in love with you and not a super model."

"But if we did get together, how long would I be able to hold your interest? We live in such different worlds; our realities are poles apart." Her words trailed off as she finished.

"Our reality is that we're both alive, here and now, and I'm madly in love with you and you have a choice to make. Take a chance with me, Corin. I can see you still want some time to grieve for Rand, but don't waste the rest of our lives. We could be good together. I'll do whatever it takes to make you happy when we're on the road. We'll find a home, wherever you want to live when we're in Boston. We'll spend as much time here as we can, if that's still what you want." They were quiet for a long time watching the sun lighten the room.

"Why is it nobody ever calls you Tommy?"

"I don't answer to it."

"Is that because it's too personal?" He held her eye and gave her a brief nod. "You responded to me this morning..."

"Damn it, Corin, that in itself should tell you something." He let out a cynical laugh and finally moved to the window seat beside her. "I'll let you call me Tommy any time you want, but first you have to tell me I'm not going to be wasting my life waiting for you when you'll never be over Rand."

"I'm not sure you really have a realistic idea of who I am, what it would be like to live with me. And quite honestly, while you were a witness to my marriage for all of three days, you have to realize that we did have our moments. Every couple does in their own way. Rand and I bickered, argued and sometimes annoyed the hell out of each other just because we existed! Tommy, marriage is work, hard work and the only thing that got us through each day, month or year was knowing that deep inside we truly loved each other." She paused to study his face. "I can be a real bitch sometimes and it isn't always associated with PMS. I'm very opinionated and stubborn to the core if I really believe in what I'm fighting for."

She hesitated and gathered her thoughts more clearly. She was trying to be honest, to get him to take off his rose-colored glasses and see reality. It only made him love her more.

"Then fight for me, Corin, fight for us." His hazel eyes bored into her. "Rand is gone and you can't get him back, ever. So keep your memories of him and fight for us. I'm not him and I'll drive you crazy just as much as he did sometimes, but in different ways. And I'll love you differently, too." His eye lashes lowered slightly, cutting off the intensity of his look. His voice went husky before he added, "I want you to be different with me, and I want to find the woman you are with me. Knowing how you loved Rand, I want the commitment and depth behind those emotions. But I want them strictly for me."

"He was my husband and I loved him very much, I always will." Tom started to turn away in defeat but she moved across to him, her fingers grabbing his chin and turning his face back to her. When she had his complete attention she went on.

"But, I'm falling in love with you and it feels very different. Different than how I loved my first husband and different again from how I loved Rand. And like I said before, the idea of falling in love with you frightens me. I don't know you enough to judge your responses, to gauge your moods to understand how your mind works. Does that make any sense to you?"

"Yes, but I consider that one of the perks of falling in love, exploring all those different paths together." She shook her head at him before pulling back.

"And my temper, my stubborn streak, you'll enjoy going down that path?"

"If it leads to making up, yes, I'll accept my due. Besides, I'm not always Mr. Personality."

"What if you decide we're not right together? What if you can't trust me any more than the first two women you married?"

"It's already different with you Corin; I really can't explain it, all I can tell you is this feels different. And it's got to be love or it wouldn't be driving me out of my mind."

"I have a feeling if we keep going like this, one day you might be sorry."

"No, only if we don't give us a chance. Do you realize our conversations automatically have us married? There's been no hedging about spending time together or a trial run living together. My intent is to have you as my wife, and you've never referred to this situation in any other way. We both see the long run ahead, Corin and we're both seeing it as permanent. You need more time..." His thumb stroked her cheek and he stood abruptly. "I'm going downstairs Corin and into a cold shower because if I don't I'm going to pull you onto one of those beds and show you just how compatible we can be together. And Corin, make no mistake, it won't be soft and kind, it will be hard and hot and all-consuming. Once we start, we won't stop."

He left her on the window seat, slightly dazed from his words. Heading towards the staircase he paused at the game table not wanting to leave her, twisting one of the handles. "Did Rand play?"

"No, it was my table. I got it as a teenager."

"Do you still play?"

"I haven't in years. Bob and I used to fool around with it once in a while."

"We're you any good?"

"I managed to win a game now and then. It's been a long time; my technique is probably pretty rusty."

"You never really lose the touch, if you had it."

"I suppose some practice would help."

"Are we still talking about foosball?"

"I'm not sure anymore," she said with a laugh and tossed the pillow towards him. He caught it easily and moved quickly back. Tom saw the flushed look on her face, her eyes wide.

"Do I scare you?" he asked.

"No," she answered a little bit too quickly, before finishing with, "I might be better off if you did." She studied him before confirming her words. "No, Tom, I'm not afraid of you, slightly intimidated perhaps, but not afraid." She held back the small smile that threatened the corners of her lips when he let out a deep, protracted breath.

"Once you're mine, Corin, we'll never let your technique get rusty again!" Tom dropped to his knees in front of her. His right hand slowly rose to her leg, his fingers barely touching as he moved them up along her thigh. Tom held her look, his hand sure of its journey. When he skimmed across her center she pulled in a breath but made no move away, nor did she take her eyes from his. She let his hand drop to cup her, watching her eyes go wide when he stroked her ever so gently.

Tom let his palm lay heavy against her, the heat from his body transferring to hers through layers of cloth.

"You're like that beautiful piano downstairs, Corin. It would be a tragic waste to put you on a shelf somewhere, only to be admired on occasion. You're an instrument I long to play, like something inside me just knows how to make you come alive." The intensity of his look didn't waver as his index finger brushed against her. "And when I finally have you Corin, I'll spend the rest of my days practicing to make you happy."

His upper body moved closer, his lips a whisper away. "I always knew in the back of my mind that you existed. I just never thought I'd get lucky enough to find you in this lifetime. Then I did, and I still couldn't have you." His lips brushed against hers and she leaned into his kiss, her hands moving slowly across his skin to his shoulders, her fingers holding him close.

The kiss changed, became urgent as did his hand against her. Corin forced the kiss, pushing against his lips, sucking his tongue deep into her warmth. He sensed she was nearing the edge. Her nails dug into his shoulders leaving small half moons in his skin as he increased his motions. She whispered only one word against his mouth, his name, "Tommy," before sliding from reality as his left arm came around to hold her to him, his fingers still dancing across her but lighter. The groan which worked its way through her was swallowed by his mouth. Tom didn't release her; he stroked her more carefully.

"You're an amazing instrument, Corin, I was born to play you, and you were born to learn me. Forget learning to play the piano, learn to play me instead. Take the rest of your life to learn how to make me yours. Teach me how to make you soar, Corin, I want the responsibility of being your safe haven. And Corin, I've never said that to any other woman. I've never wanted the responsibility before, but from you, your trust..."

****

Corin lay against his chest, slightly embarrassed and extremely sated. When she finally spoke, it wasn't what she thought she might say. "Damn you, Tommy Hayden," she started but never finished, her hands moved up his neck, pulling his head towards her. She took his mouth in an unrelenting storm of passion and need, somewhat stunned when he pulled away to stare at her.

"Corin, I'm going downstairs or there'll be no other options. It's not my first choice but when we're finally together I want just you and me in the room." He slowly eased her back against the cushions and pulled away.

Obviously chilled, he watched the shiver run through her; not stopping his impulse to drop his mouth towards her chest. A slight tug on the zipper of her sweatshirt had her bared to him. His eyes studied her as he dropped his mouth to take first one berried bud then the other gently between his lips.

She gasped at the warmth he brought her and her hands instinctively moved towards him. Her left hand captured the back of his head, her fingers threading through his hair as she held him to her breast. With her right, Corin captured his hardened length, felt the denim stretched to its seams and sighed again. He overflowed her palm and she felt him surge against her slight movements.

Tom lifted his head and brought his moist lips to hers engulfing her in another round of longing kisses that had them both breathing hard. Tom managed to find the piece of mind to pull completely away from her when he realized he was moving against her hand, each small motion an exquisite torture.

"Damn it, Corin, I can't keep my hands off you." He stepped away, his hands threading through his blonde hair. "I've got to get away from here or..." Tom bent down and grabbed the pillow from the floor where he'd tossed it.

"Or?" she managed to ask.

"Or we both know I'll wind up imbedded inside you. Do I leave or stay, Corin?"

She had no answer, all she could do was stare, knowing if he touched her one more time she'd never let him go. He dropped the pillow on her lap and left her wild-eyed, half-aroused and only half sated. Left her wanting to answer him but she was too flustered to find the words. He left her wanting to check out the rest of his technique in the worst way. Corin stayed where she was for a long time, moving only when she heard noise from the spare rooms below her.

****

Breakfast was in the final steps when he appeared in the kitchen later that morning. Corin pressed a mug of hot coffee into his hand, whispered, "Good morning," and continued her conversation with Anna.

"Put them through on my e-mail, but send me the hard copies, all right?" Anna only nodded as Joe entered the room. Whatever the subject was, they weren't going to talk about it any more. Before Tom could comprehend, they'd finished their meal and the truck was packed. Corin hadn't changed out of her sweats and he fought the urge to tug the zipper down one last time, to take one last taste and sight of her firm breasts presenting themselves.

There were hugs and thanks in several rounds, invitations to swim and boat in the warmer weather; Corin reassuring both Joe and Anna their visit had been most welcome. While the ground was starting to dry out, it was still too wet to attempt a major clean up and they had no choice. The rest of the tour was waiting for them to get back. She'd packed them a cooler full of food but he hadn't watched, instead he remembered the snack she packed him the last time he left her home.

"Thank you for coming down," she said carefully as he was about to move into the driver's seat.

"I wish I'd have been able to do more." They both smiled at his double meanings.

"I think you did quite enough. I know the time is

getting nearer that I return some of your kindness."
If Joe or Anna understood their undercurrent
neither let on.

Tom abandoned all restraint and grabbed her,
wrapping his arms tightly around her before burying
his face in her short curly hair. She molded against
him, not caring what his friends thought.

"Damn it, Tommy," she whispered.

"Some day, Corin, I won't leave you, I promise."

"I'm going to hold you to that promise..." He
caught her look and laughed lightly.

"Don't look so daunted, it's not a prison
sentence."

"No, it's becoming my reality. What will you do
when it becomes yours?"

"I'll thank the powers that be that brought us
together. And I won't let you go Corin. Know that,
once you're mine..."

"In a strange way I think a part of me has
always been yours, even before I knew you existed."

"You have a copy of the schedule and you know
how to get in touch with me. We've got a few breaks
coming up, why not get things settled here and come
up to Boston. I could show you around a little, let
you get a feel for the city."

"I'll think about it."

"That's better than automatically ruling it out.
I'll take what you can give me for the time being."
Tom kissed Corin without hesitating. He didn't care
that Anna and Joe were watching. He wanted one
last memory of her, understanding it would be a long
time before he saw her again.

Corin managed to pull back and sent them on
their way before the morning traffic mounted.

****

When they turned out of her driveway Tom
couldn't resist asking the question he most wanted
answered. "Anna, how badly damaged was her

studio?"

She leaned forward between the two front seats, her right hand dropping on Joe's shoulder as she spoke. "The back wall was saturated from a roof leak but the limb missed the skylight. Most of her canvases were stacked in the living room and her supplies were all moved out of the way. Mostly it seemed she caught it in time, if she hadn't been here it would have been much worse. And the portrait of Rand, if that had been damaged..."

"She's working on his portrait?"

"Yes. Was I not supposed to tell you that?"

"No, it's fine. How far along is it?" He tried to sound nonchalant and didn't manage it, only affirming to his friends the implications of the particular picture.

"About three quarters..." He let out a sigh and neither Joe or Anna remarked any further, instead Anna went on to tell him about the watercolor series she was getting ready to ship to the Soho gallery.

"Did she mention which one?"

"No, not that I can remember, just a small place in Soho." When he didn't question her further, she pushed back in the seat.

Tom had driven several miles north of Wilmington when Joe asked the fatal question. He mentioned hearing music last night, a haunting melody he'd never heard before. From that one question, Tom finally told him about the song. He knew by sharing it now it was a leap of faith and he hoped he wasn't wrong. Deep inside, this felt right; especially knowing Corin was working on Rand's portrait.

The one he'd seen of her mother had been her way of healing and he hoped this meant the same thing; she was finding perspective and getting ready to move forward. It was automatic for Anna to reach behind her seat and hand Joe the guitar he never went anywhere without when he asked her for it. Anna asked Tom to stop at the gas station a few minutes later. While Tom automatically got out to top off the tank, Anna used the time to slip behind the steering wheel.

"You can't drive and compose at the same time," she said with a smile. "And your mind is on," she hesitated; Tom knew she'd almost said Corin then changed it to "the song, not the road."

Tom accepted her opinion and slipped into the back seat, rummaging around in his bag for something to write on. The rest of their trip went quickly. Anna drove while Tom and Joe roughed out the rest of the ballad. By the time they made it to Virginia Beach, he knew the song would be a hit. And he knew one day he'd tell Corin about their drive and how it all came together.

From that time on, Tom Hayden felt more like himself than he had in a long time. Since last winter everyone had noticed a change in him, he was sullen and withdrawn. After seeing Corin something inside him changed. He began to feel like he was on the right road, finally. Everyone around him seemed thankful it was for the better.

Chapter Eleven

"You certainly left me with a lot to think about," she teased later that night with the phone cradled to her ear. She scraped supper remnants into Beau's bowl and mixed in dry kibble. He danced around beside her, letting out several low, off-key howling like sounds.

"What are you doing to the poor dog?"

"Just getting his supper ready," she answered, placing the bowl near the utility hall. He almost pushed her down to get to it. "Jeez, you'd think the dog never got a meal before."

"Not possible in your house."

"Was the ride back awful? You must be exhausted?"

"Tired, but productive, I finally shared the song with Joe; we worked on it during the drive."

"While you were driving?"

"No, Anna took the wheel."

"Remind me to thank her for that," she teased. "Tom, what made you decide to share it? Last night you told me you wouldn't."

"I know, but I realized if I had faith in both of us...the song...I suppose it was my way of telling the world I'm in love with you."

"Oh," she managed, confused by his approach.

"Corin, answer one question for me, please?"

"Sure, what?"

"This weekend I didn't see your wedding ring..."

"It was a conscious decision Tom. I stopped wearing it last month when our phone calls started. I realized it was..."

How could she ever explain the emotions that went with that very act? She couldn't and didn't try, to remember would be counterproductive to the future she was trying to build for herself. She'd known from the start she had to find herself before moving on to another relationship.

"Corin?"

"I realized I had no right to wear his ring and fantasize about you."

"Thank you," he said quietly. Dead air hung between them but it didn't seem uncomfortable.

Finally Corin started laughing. "That one left you speechless," she teased.

"Yes, it did."

"Are you ready to get back to the tour?"

"Time moves quicker if I'm busy. My mind doesn't wander as much..."

"I know that feeling."

"Corin, think about taking a few days with me, just to get the feel of touring."

"I got a feel of things this morning, all right." Corin laughed at her own words before adding, "It just wasn't a long enough caress."

"Any longer and we'd still be in your attic." His words hit her as if he'd struck her and she knew he was right. If he'd stayed with her any longer, she would have given herself to him freely and greedily taken all he could offer her.

"I should let you go, get some sleep. Pleasant dreams, Tom. Thanks for coming down to see me."

"I couldn't stay away. So tell me, you've had all day to think about what we talked about. Are you going to tell me to never call again?" His resigned tone made her think it was one of his fears.

"No. Having second thoughts?"

"Try tenth and eleventh. But not about us, only what I want to happen when we're finally together."

"What if I disappoint you?" She'd thought about

that all afternoon while trying to set the studio back to rights. The storm had forced her to clean out the space at the same time. When she was comfortable with the end result, she realized she'd not only cleaned it but changed the whole atmosphere in the space. Everything that had been collecting on her walls for the last seven years was gone, carefully stored away. Bright white walls looked back at her, only a few canvases remained in the living room with her charcoals and pastels. Her paints had been packed until the repairs were completed. The whole time she wondered if she could live up to his expectations, whatever they might be.

"That would never happen, Corin."

"I'm going to ask a favor of you Tom." She heard him draw a breath and tried to reassure him. "Please, don't panic, all right? I'm just asking for some time to get my act together." She hesitated before being brutally honest with him. "Whatever you planned to accomplish with your visit you surely went beyond."

"What are you trying to tell me?"

"That all afternoon I've been longing for you, for your touch and your taste, and all afternoon I had to keep reminding myself that I'd only lost my husband months ago." Corin waited for a response but pushed ahead when he was quiet. "I cleaned the studio this afternoon, Tom. Stripped it bare, stored everything away but paint and blank canvas."

"A fresh start?" he questioned.

"Yes, but it wasn't like I planned to do it, it just happened. I went to straighten it out after shifting things from the storm and one thing led to the other and the room was blank. And that's kind of how I need to feel right now. Does that make any sense?"

"I'm not sure," he told her truthfully.

"Tom, I'm asking you for some time to strip out the rest of my cobwebs."

"Are you telling me not to call you again or just that you need time?"

"I need to find who I am at this point in my life before I can commit to you. I know who I was with Ted and why. And I knew who I was with Rand. But now, I'm not sure who I've become."

"The woman I love," he told her wholeheartedly.

"I don't know her yet," Corin told him. "I need to find her on my own."

"How can I help? I'd be willing to lend a hand any way you'd like." His voice conveyed more than he said outright. She laughed at his remark.

"That's just it, Tom. The woman who let you touch her this morning, I don't understand her. We don't know each other yet I let you...and what scares me more is what I wanted to do to you." Clearing her throat she finished. "I realized showing you the nudes was an intimate act."

"God, Corin, you can't tell me something like that and expect me to back off."

"It's the only way, Tom. Give me some time, please?"

"Of course, but I don't have to like it."

"That old stubborn streak inside me..."

"Corin, take the time you need, but know whatever you find at the end of your journey, I'll still love you and deep down you know you care about me."

"Yes, I do." When she spoke again it was to change the subject. "I've made plans to go to Florida for Christmas. My dad called this afternoon and Tom, I think he's dating. He didn't come right out and say so, but I think he has a lady friend."

"How do you feel about that?"

"I'm not sure. I never really thought about it before. But he's been alone so long, over ten years. I just want him to be happy."

"And Christmas?"

"Is a means to an end? I'll drive down with Beau and spend a few weeks. And most likely meet my stepmother-to-be." She laughed and relaxed.

"What else did you decide this afternoon?"

"That I have to clean out Rand's things from the house, at least pack his office. As you saw, I've already started to reclaim the bedroom."

"Just because you empty his side of the closet doesn't mean you'll forget him."

"I know that, but can you live with the reality of it?"

"I have to. He'll always be your second husband. As long as I'm the third and the last, got it?"

"We'll see. I'm going to back away for a while, Tom. Don't read anything sinister into it, all right? I just need to do this for myself."

"I don't see any alternative that won't piss you off, so all right for now."

"Thank you for understanding."

****

Understanding and liking it were two completely different matters. He'd hung up the phone and knew he couldn't call her, at least for a while. She'd asked for time to mourn her husband and find herself in the process. She'd do it on her own time frame. Somehow in the back of his mind he knew he wouldn't hear much from her until next spring. It was going to be a long winter for Tom Hayden.

Christmas afternoon he'd gone to Anna and Joe's as arranged. The girls were thrilled with their gifts from Uncle Tom and were hesitant to leave the adults alone after a late lunch. Several members from both sides of their family were in residence for the celebration and Joe often told Tom he was a great buffer to his relatives, a role they'd reversed all through their relationship. Anna brought Tom's attention to a portrait of the twins leaning against the wall behind the Christmas tree. He'd glimpsed it earlier and tried to look at it several times but kept getting interrupted.

"What do you think, Tom?" The adults were scattered around the family room, the television on but basically being ignored. Joe played a new guitar Anna had made for him while his parents played cards with hers. The girls were lying before the fireplace, a new board game spread out before them. She brought the wood framed picture towards him. Matted with a linen border, it was the twins, preserved in a light-hearted moment of time. The artist had captured the subtle differences between them but also saw the sameness. It was a beautiful portrait in pastels. He didn't need to study it long; he knew who the artist was.

"Corin..." he whispered to himself but Anna agreed. She went on to tell him about sending down some photos and getting this just a week ago. They'd apparently discussed the idea when they were in her studio last September and Anna hadn't told Joe. When he glanced towards them he smiled.

"Amazing, isn't it. She's made them angelic yet caught the hint of mischief."

"Yes," was all he managed to say, so many questions swirled inside him. As if she could read his mind, Anna continued.

"When I didn't hear anything back for a long time I figured she'd decided against it. But then here it was." She took it back towards the stacked presents and carefully leaned it against the wall, propping it carefully. "I tried to call to thank her but got a machine, so I e-mailed her. I haven't heard anything back."

"She was planning on going to see her dad for the holidays," Tom contributed.

He left shortly after dessert, thankful for the meal and company and even more thankful to get away. Joe met him at the door as he pulled on his coat, a large box in his hands.

"This was in the same crate with a note to get it to you. Anna figured you'd rather not open it with an audience." Tom took the parcel and gauged its weight in his hands.

"Thanks," he managed and than added, "Tell Anna she has good instincts. I'll talk to you next week; enjoy the rest of your time with the family."

"Thanks, I'll see you next week."

****

Tom was thankful to get away and even more thankful he made it home in record time. The package now sat propped on his bed. Tom had come home and opened a bottle of wine before jumping in a hot shower. He'd put off the inevitable as long as possible, the tips of his fingers all but itching to tear at the gold foil paper. A small white envelope was taped to the corner, just his name written in Corin's bold printing. Slipping it from its sleeve he studied the winter scene on the front of the card; a shore line, snow covering the beach. In the dark sky above it, one star shone brightly. He was hesitant to read her words, afraid of them being a total kiss off. The words to his ballad struck him and he opened it before thinking further.

"Dear Tom,

I've been thinking about you.

I hope you have a merry Christmas and a better New Year."

She'd signed it, Corin. No sincerely or love, just Corin.

He placed the card on the side table, finished the wine in his glass and then pulled the package forward. Tearing the wrapping away he stood stunned, and too astonished to react immediately. The charcoal portrait was of him. He knew the look she'd captured. He'd been intent on what he was doing, probably playing the piano. Or hollering at her, he thought with a laugh. Then he realized the look and knew she'd drawn him as she saw him that last morning in the attic. His mind echoed the way her voice whispered his name. Whatever moment she'd chosen, the intensity in his eyes amazed him. She'd matted it in a dark brown and used a dark wood frame around it. Tom propped it against his pillows and walked around the room, staring at it from all angles.

****

He hadn't known what to do, whether to ignore the holidays or not. His first impulse was to send her jewelry which he knew would be wrong. In the end, Bob had reluctantly given him her father's Florida address and he'd shipped down the two cookie jars he'd found online. He hoped she liked them and knew she didn't have ones similar to them in her kitchen collection. Tom wondered if the symbolism behind them would be lost and laughed. Corin would get it, because she got him. Somehow they didn't seem near enough compared to the present she sent him. Dialing before he could change his mind or worry about the late hour, her cell phone rang only twice before she answered it.

"Hi, Merry Christmas," she said, her voice light with laughter.

"Merry Christmas, Corin," he managed and heard her swift intake of air.

"Hi, how are you? I got your presents, Tom. Thank you for remembering me." She hesitated then laughed again before asking, "Are the wolf and little red riding hood a metaphor?" He laughed aloud and they both relaxed.

"At times since I met you I've felt akin to the wolf."

"At times since I met you I've felt akin with red riding hood!"

"Well, at least we both understand each other. I never meant to be predatory, never have been before, but you, Corin, make me feel voracious at times." She laughed and the sound of her voice warmed him. "Corin, your laughter is the best Christmas present I've gotten."

"You're easy to please," she stopped, "No, I take that back, you're not easy at all. You're a very complex man, Mr. Hayden. But, I'll give you this, I love the cookie jars and I'll display them with pride, but, the best part was the candy inside them."

Tom had filled both the jars with miniature versions of her favorite candy bars. Three kinds were mixed in each jar and he instantly remembered tearing open the candy bags and dumping them on the desk, blending the flavors before filling each container.

"My first instinct was to fill them with Godiva chocolate but I remembered overhearing you at Sunday supper telling Mrs. Larsen if you ate Godiva all the time you wouldn't appreciate it."

"You heard that?"

"Yeah."

"But you buried a bar of Godiva in the center of each jar?"

"Just for a special treat."

"Thank you, Tommy," Corin whispered.

"How was the rest of you're tour and what about you're Christmas?" She went on with several more questions before running out of steam. "Tom?"

"I don't know which one to answer first," he told her, and knew she relaxed on the other end of the phone. "I miss you, Corin. I managed to hold off calling all this time, but you'll never know how hard it was. I love my present, it's...It brought tears to my eyes. I knew you were talented, but you managed to make even me look human."

"And intense..."

"And sexual..."

"That too, but that's how I see you. You are intense and extremely sexual."

"Only to you."

"I sincerely doubt that."

"Are you all right?"

"I'm getting better," she told him before adding, "I don't see any way around it. Either I fight for myself or I'll wither away with only memories."

"Memories should be just that, put away for an occasional re-visit. What you need to do is start making new ones."

"And they should include you?"

"Of course." They'd taken a serious turn and he didn't want to leave the conversation quite so somber.

"So, is your stepmother to be a witch or not?"

Corin laughed at his tactic and went on to tell him she'd met a very nice, slightly older than middle-aged retired school teacher originally from New Jersey who was widowed five years earlier. Their conversation stalled, Corin broke the impasse.

"Tom, I finished Rand's portrait at Thanksgiving. I sent it to his mother."

"I don't know what to say," Tom admitted.

"You don't have to say anything; I just wanted you to understand I'd finished his before I started yours."

"It shouldn't matter, but it does. Thank you for telling me."

When they finally disconnected it was with the promise she'd call him New Years Day. He wasn't happy with her time frame but a week was a whole lot better than three months.

He'd had several invitations to parties and gatherings but declined them all. Somehow the idea of spending New Year's Eve with a group wasn't appealing. He stayed home, alone. At midnight he thought to call Corin and changed his mind several times before it was too late to actually make the call. The day stretched out before him, sports on the television and too much quiet around him. He kept the cell phone near him all day, hoping it would ring. It was after nine when it finally did.

"Hi, Happy New Year," she started, her voice light.

"Hi." Tom had wanted to talk to her for so long and now his mind went blank. All the little things he stored up to use as conversation were gone from his mind. "How bad was it?" he said before thinking.

"I survived, but then we knew I would, it's just a matter of time."

"Are you still with your Dad?"

"No, I drove home mid-week. I had to get through this one here. I can't explain it, only that it felt right."

"Was it cleansing for you?"

"I suppose. I hadn't thought of it from that perspective, only that if I didn't come home it would defeat me somehow." They managed to dance around what they both wanted to say for a long time, sharing bits of holiday stories. "I don't think my Dad will get married soon, although not because they don't want to. It seems a shame for them to lose benefits and pensions if they do. It's like being penalized for falling in love when you're over sixty five."

"They'll work it out between them," Tom told her.

"That's the only way it will work. I liked her, and she made Dad laugh again."

"What about you, Corin? What would make you laugh again?"

"I'm working on that, too."

"When can I see you?" he boldly asked.

"Soon," she whispered, adding, "If you still want

to?"

"Any time, all the time, Corin."

"I'll get back to you in a while, Tom. Take care of yourself."

With a few simple words he knew he'd not hear from her for a while. On one hand he understood her on the other the concept annoyed him on many levels. Never had he let a woman rule any relationship, especially a sexual one, until now. It made him feel whipped from one perspective, and still allowed her control. That in itself was enough to reinforce he'd gone crazy. He'd fallen in love with Corin and until she was ready his life would stay in a state of flux. Not a good place for any person to be.

Chapter Twelve

The enormity of the situation almost overwhelmed him. All day the air around him hummed with a strange static he'd been unable to identify other than the third weekend in February, Presidents weekend. Pushing open the hotel room door he knew immediately someone had been in his room. The lights were off; several candles placed on the bureau the only lighting. Miles Davis played in the background instead of the television he always left on. In the far corner of the room, standing before the sliding glass door with her back to him was his salvation. Closing the door softly behind him he leaned back against it and tried to gulp for air. Suddenly he felt like a teenager about to go on his first date.

Corin turned slowly, her hair longer on her shoulders again, the candle light reflecting blonde and red highlights. She wore a long plaid flannel shirt in green tartan. Several sizes too large, the hem hanging at the back of her knees, the sleeves rolled back several times and still falling about her wrists. Thick cotton socks covered her feet. Using her left hand, she pushed the curls from her face and Tom felt instantly relieved there was still no ring, resolving to change that as soon as she'd let him. He couldn't speak, couldn't find his voice let alone come up with something coherent. She broke the trance.

"Is this a mistake?" she asked. Tom let out a breath and smiled.

"Not if you're real and not a figment of my imagination."

"I'm real, Tom." She moved towards him slowly, studying him, watching him. Tom felt stripped naked from her look. "As real as you want me to be..." She reached him still standing with his back to the door. Taking his jacket and card key from his hands, she dropped them on the counter beside them before she reached behind him and put the second lock on the door. Then she stood back, just inches from him, studying him.

Her hands slipped up along his chest, coming to rest behind his head. He held her gaze, refusing to break the contact, physical and emotional. His large hands skimmed against her waist, tightening around her and pulling her up against his body, his arousal unable to be hidden. She understood and moved gently against him.

"How?" he whispered, still holding her over his erection.

"Does it matter?" she whispered back. "Ask me later," she said just before she reached up onto her toes to take his mouth with hers. She let her lips hover above his then pulled back. "Whatever happens in this room..."

"Never leaves here, except in my memory." From that moment on all attempts at sane thinking were gone. Tom lifted her from the floor, his fingers tightening around her waist and holding her against him. Automatically her legs locked around him. Corin's fingers were wrapped behind his head, his hair tangled with them. She used them to direct his mouth where she wanted him for better access. Long and slow, she teased his lips, learned his shape and savored his taste. All the while she kept moving rhythmically around him.

Tom tried to take control of their position and the kiss but didn't succeed; he surrendered to Corin's wants, letting her explore him at her own pace. When she broke away for air his head dropped back against the door, his breathing labored. Her tongue was running along his chin, down his throat along his neck. Her fingers fell forward and started to unbutton his shirt. He shifted her weight and she smiled up.

"Hello, Tom," she whispered against his neck.

"Hello, Corin," he managed, then added, "I've been waiting for you." He dropped his mouth over hers and turned them around, her back now pressed against the wood. Her eyes betrayed what he interpreted as a small flash of surprise and he smiled before taking control. His kiss was demonstrative and Corin gave in to his want, letting him kiss her until she felt weak against his arms, her sigh swallowed by his mouth. Finally he pulled back, his look intense and questioning.

"I suppose if you put me down I could get you undressed quicker," she teased; suddenly they were both laughing, relaxing with each other. He moved a few steps and let her bottom down on top of the counter, leaving her sitting with her legs still stretched around his thighs. The mirror behind them reflected their images. Her fingers undid each button, the process agonizingly slow.

He watched her with a detached fascination and she smiled. "I'm real Tom," she told him as she pulled his shirt from his pants, pushing the garment off his shoulders. Her fingers moved to the cotton shirt underneath and dragged it up over his belly, her nails leaving a light pattern with the movement. He closed his eyes to savor the moment, to memorize the feel of her hands on his skin for the first time.

"Tell me what you want?" he said as he took a half step back and pulled the shirt up over his head and off, tossing it in the general direction of the bed. He started to unbutton her shirt and decided against it, instead he pulled her arms up and tugged the shirt off over her head, tossing it with the rest of his discarded clothing. Tom sighed aloud when he finally got a good look at her. She wore a silky white camisole that matched her bikini bottoms. His hands slid along her torso, stopping to cup her, to mold his hands around her. Again he said, "Tell me what you want."

"Everything, of course, did you think this would be easy?" Her teeth scraped along his bare shoulder, her fingers traced his ribs. "I want whatever you can give me and I plan to take everything I can." Her tongue found his nipple and drew a light path over it. Her fingers taunted his stomach before slowly pushing the leather of his belt through the buckle, pausing to pull it from the loops before tossing it on the floor near his shirt.

Corin went back to using her lips against his skin while his fingers laced behind her head, pulling her attention back to his mouth. She opened to him, accepted him and sparred for more.

Tom slid his hands along her arms, down to her legs. It was no effort for him to slip them between her thighs. He felt the heat of her skin against his and sucked her bottom lip into his mouth; this action combined with his fingers finding her heated core made her groan, advancing her hips against his hand. He cupped her easily, the thin silk panties no barrier. The moist material moved out of his way and let him slip between her lips, her natural heat prompting him to explore her further.

He moved his left hand higher, cupping the curve of her breast, taking its weight in his palm, rolling her nipple between his thumb and index finger. She budded at his touch, responded by dragging her hands along his waist until she found the button on his jeans. She slipped it open but didn't go further letting her hand drop and cupped him similarly as he held her. He throbbed in her palm and she smiled up at him.

"I don't seem to be having much luck getting you out of these clothes..."

"We'll get there," he told her through gritted teeth as her fingers pulsed around him. She went slick under his hand, his finger slipping easily inside her. She stilled above him for long seconds, and then slowly moved over his invasion, accepting what he offered. She dragged her hands to his face, turning him back to her and sucked his tongue deep into her mouth, matching the rhythm of his finger. She was hot and ready and his first impulse was to take her there, against the counter.

"Corin..." he managed to utter when he stopped her kiss. He stilled his hand over her and she looked at him through lowered lashes. "Darlin', if we don't get off this counter, I'm going to take you here."

"Take me, Tom, right here, right now. The rest can wait, I can't. I want to feel you inside me, please..."

Her hands pulled away and carefully lowered his zipper then pushed the rest of the material down his hips, taking him into her hand. She stroked him lightly, learning the feel of him, full in her small hand. Her nails lightly dragged against his shaft and he drew a quick breath.

"Corin..."

"Here Tommy, now." She watched as his fingers tore the cloth from her crotch. He took a half step forward and pulled her hips up, plunging inside her in one smooth, unfettered motion. When he buried to the limit he paused, stunned by his action. Corin's eyes were closed; her head dropped back on her shoulders, her hair a tangle of curls around her face falling onto the counter. Her mouth was open to a perfect oval. He pulsed inside her when he thought about the possibilities.

Only then did he start to slowly move inside her, his motions mostly interior rather than large exterior moves. Corin used her own muscles to challenge him back, taking his face in her hands, pulling it towards her mouth, watching him intently as he pushed her towards the edge of reason.

She responded by taking each stroke and tightening further. Tom kept her tight against him with his right hand, using his left to find her breast; smiling when he found her nipples budded at attention. He dropped his mouth to cover her and he knew she felt his light nips even through the silk. With each touch of his teeth against her nipple she clenched internally around him. He knew his reserve was fading fast, pulling from her breast and grabbing her hips, tightening her higher against him. She gasped and he felt her go slick around him, heat draining against him. It was too much and he finally let himself go; taking the last few thrusts for him.

Corin crumpled against him; her legs quivering at his thighs while she made small internal movements around him. He groaned and dropped his head to her shoulder.

"Welcome home, Corin." Her hands were making lazy patterns on his bare back and she chuckled against his chest.

"It's nice to be here," she told him in all seriousness, before adding, "But I didn't manage to get you out of these clothes yet, Mr. Hayden."

"What would you suggest?" he asked, his teeth nipping at her earlobe.

"How about, I'll give you a glass of wine and a few minutes to catch your breath and then you're in trouble?"

"What kind of trouble?" He sucked the soft skin of her neck into his mouth, his tongue running a pattern against it. She quaked against him and tightened her legs around him once more.

"I'll think of something..." was all she managed

before he silenced her with his kiss.

****

They did make it to the bed and eventually lost the rest of their clothes, the layers being stripped away in hurried movements to feel skin against skin. Tom took one look at Corin stretched naked across the large bed and took her with a force he hadn't known he possessed. What surprised him more was Corin's raspy whispers.

"Faster, Tommy, deeper, harder...there, right there." She clenched around him a second time causing him to lose his restraint. He pulled from inside her and dropped onto the bed next to her, his breathing returning to a normal pattern.

"Damn it, Corin, I had all these wonderful fantasies of a slow seduction and peeling away your clothes, exploring you as I went. Yet the minute I saw you..." He turned on his side, his hand reaching to stroke her hip as he spoke.

"You promised me wine," he teased and let his fingers dip lower to caress her belly, following the contours of skin until his fingers ran along her scar line, much smaller and lighter than he'd been prepared for. He traced it several times before moving his touch higher and lower. She shuddered under his exploration and rolled away laughing.

"I promised you wine..." she said and reluctantly moved from his side. "You can seduce me later." She went to the compact refrigerator and pulled out the bottle she apparently stashed earlier. Using the glass tumblers provided, she deftly opened the wine and tossed the cork screw back into her bag.

When she brought him his glass, she slipped beside him, lying on her side facing him.

"Thank you for coming to me." He touched his glass against hers before taking a long sip from it. "Can I ask how and why now?" She smiled over the rim of her glass.

"How was with Joe and Anna's help. I phoned them earlier this morning and asked if they thought this was a good or bad time. Joe said we should let you decide for yourself and made arrangements to leave a key at the desk for me."

"Were you at the show?"

"No." He studied her and waited for her to continue. "I wanted to be with you, the man, not the performer or musician. Tonight, I just wanted to be waiting for you when you came home from work."

"And why now, because it's the third weekend of the month? I assumed you'd be having Sunday supper this week. I left a message on your home machine earlier today."

"I know I checked them earlier." She smiled and handed him her glass, her hands taking long slow passes over his stomach and thighs, just missing the obvious target. "I stopped having Sunday suppers this past year. It just wasn't the same, too painful in the first few months after Rand died, and then I just never wanted to do it again. You can't go back and all that..." She let her fingers dance over him, to softly caress him only occasionally while she stroked the rest of his torso. "The now is because it felt right, because I hadn't left the house in too long and had an excuse to be in Texas."

"What excuse?"

"I got a call a few weeks back from an old business acquaintance. He asked me if I could help out with a project out here. I was about to turn him down and decided it wouldn't hurt to see what he was describing. When they agreed to wait until this week for me to travel it seemed a good reason to come. I couldn't disappear for a week without raising a few eyebrows, mainly Dad's and Bob's. So this little business trip was a good excuse." She took her glass from his hand and sipped before rolling to the side and putting it on the table. "I didn't have to lie to anyone about my whereabouts and basically just didn't tell them my complete itinerary."

"And if you hadn't gotten the call?" She turned from him and retrieved her glass.

"Corin?"

"I'd been thinking about coming to see you. Thinking this weekend would be appropriate somehow. When the job turned out to be in Santa Fe, Dallas was just a short flight away. I decided the fates were sending me a message."

"Thank God for fate." Tom moved from beside her and put his glass aside. He tugged her against him, half under him, his leg dropping over hers. "Are you going to take the job?" He had to know, had to find out what direction she was thinking in.

"No. I never planned on it. I just gave them some idea of what it would take to restore it and mainly impressed upon them what not to do until they got a professional restorer on site." She laughed and he relaxed.

"What was it, a painting?"

"No, a wall of frescoes in a small church outside the city. It had been discovered during some renovations. It was beautiful, Tom, so simple yet so complex. From the records the church was able to find, the last renovation was in the early nineteen twenties. We figure that's when they plastered over it. It must be at least fifty or sixty years earlier than that. Whoever works on it will date it."

"And you're fingers weren't itching to get to work on it?"

"Surprisingly, no. It would mean staying in Santa Fe for at least a year, if not longer. My fingers were itching for something, but it wasn't the fresco. It was you, Tom. All this time I've been trying to reconcile how I could love Rand so deeply yet have this want for you at the same time. Once I accepted the fact that I'd never get him back, no matter what,

I found perspective. I finally allowed myself to admit I've fallen for you. Once I did that, I had to see you, had to know if it was real or just..."

"Or just?" His fingers found her damp curls and started stroking them lightly.

"Or just...I had to know if this was real or if I'd fabricated these feelings because I wanted them."

"No fabrication, Corin, I've wanted you from the moment I walked into your foyer and saw you for the first time. And I never thought I'd be so lucky to actually have you lying beside me. Here in Dallas or anywhere else." Their kiss sealed their fate.

****

Hours later after a shower and room service, Corin lay in Tom's arms.

"How long?" he whispered as he pulled her closer to his chest, his arms locked around her.

"Well, if it's not a problem, I thought you might be able to get me in to see your show tomorrow night. You move on the morning after to Phoenix, I have a flight home the same time. So, unless you're tired of me already, I'd say you're stuck with me until it's time to leave Dallas. Can you cope with that or am I being too forward, expecting too much too soon?" Her hand dropped to his crotch and simply held him.

"I'll accept anything you give me, for now. But after the..."

"Go ahead, tell me what you were about to say, please Tom." She pulled from his side and looked down at him, not moving her hand.

"I was about to say after the anniversaries I wanted you with me full time. And I hesitated because I didn't want to bring up bad memories right now."

"Thank you. But let's get something straight, right from the beginning." She waited until he gave her his full attention before going on. "I can't change my history, Tom, nobody can. So at times there will be memories or references to the accident, to Ted and even to Rand. I can't erase any of it. All I can tell you is that they're in their place in my mind. And while I'll always be sad about all three things for very different reasons, if I'm to have any happiness in the future I've had to let them go. You have to decide if you can too."

"There will be references to my two ex-wives too."

"I know. And while I won't like hearing about them any more than you'll like hearing mention of Rand or Ted, it's a reality we have to live with."

"As long as I'm living with you, I'll handle it."

She tightened her grip on him and he pulsed in her palm. "Then let me handle this for a while, you relax." She moved down his body and used slow motions with her hands and lips to explore him, learn him, making him hers in this intimate way. He groaned softy.

"Tommy," she said, than paused to take him with her mouth for several strokes before finishing her thought. "I finally found home," she managed to tell him, just before engulfing him whole.

****

Tom kept her close all day, his arm or hand always on her. He introduced her to everyone without a second thought, yet Corin realized several of the introductions were tense, his fingers tightening around her waist or hand; as if he was warning these particular people. She was his and that was the end of it. Most of the crew and back up musicians seemed surprised to meet her, but because they'd had no idea she existed. His demonstrative displays eased during the day when he saw how people reacted to her and how she interacted with them.

In the time before they were to take the stage,

he watched her with Joe's daughters. She was natural with them, comfortable even though they'd never met. The sight made him long for something he never thought to want, his own children. The realization struck him on many levels. The idea had crossed his mind since meeting her, but now it solidified. Watching her, he wanted his own family, as long as she was beside him. With Corin as their mother, his children would be blessed. Forcing himself, he shook off the idea, knowing the odds of it ever happening weren't on his side. But the reality of it made him see that as long as she was with him, they'd do all right together.

****

Tom felt different when he came off the stage, focused and intent. While he'd been near her all day something had shifted between them this evening, he didn't know just what. In the back seat of the car on the way back to the hotel, he let his head drop back against the seat, his hand holding hers between them. Once they got back to his room, he seemed higher strung than ever. Corin walked in ahead of him and dropped her purse on the desk, her suede jacket following it. When she turned back he was staring from the doorway.

"Tom?" He stared at her but didn't move or answer.

She moved towards him, watching his face for a sign. "What's wrong?" With several feet still between them he let his eyes close against the sight of her. "Tom, talk to me, please?" Her fingers reached to his jaw, angling him to look directly at her. "Tell me?" He only groaned and let his head drop back against the door. "Did I do something wrong, should I leave?"

He heard the tremor in her voice and caught her against him with too much force. He felt the air rush from her lungs, the surprise on her face apparent.

"The only thing wrong is that in twelve hours

you'll be gone." She relaxed against him, her hands going around his neck.

"Then we'd better take advantage of those hours while we have them." Her lips drew along his chin, down his throat and she dropped her hand between them.

"I'm on a short leash just now, Corin." His words were tight; he was fighting some internal demand for control.

"Take the leash off, Tom. I'm not afraid of you." Her hand held him tighter and he watched her intently. "You're angry with me, that much I can see, but I'm not sure why."

"Not angry..."

"Yes, you are upset, why?" She continued to hold him against the door, not letting him drop the point. Corin watched several emotions wash over him yet he didn't share any of them. He dropped his head to take her mouth under his. It was a possessive kiss, taking not giving.

"God help us, Corin," he whispered, just before he took her in his arms and turned her back to the door. His hands held hers tight against the wood while his mouth continued to tell her what he wanted. When she tried to move to touch him, he took both her wrists and drew them over her head, anchoring them both with his left hand. His right hand slowly dropped down, tracing the outline of her face and neck before coming in contact with her shirt. In one movement, he tore the front open; buttons popping in different directions as he bared her to him. Her bra released with the flick of his index finger on the front clasp.

Corin drew a breath when he tore her shirt open and she accepted his frustration. He wanted to punish her for making him wait. His lips found her nipple while his fingers crushed her breast under their weight. She sighed under his attentions and it only fueled him to go further. There was no discussion, he simply let go of her arms, his look warned her not to move. No conversation passed between them; instead she took what he offered.

Tom managed to open her jeans with a minimum of wasted movements, pushing them and her panties down her hips, his hand dropping to cover her, his finger testing her path, finding it hot and ready. He pushed inside her and she shut her eyes against his invasion. For several seconds neither of them moved. Then he slowly moved his finger inside her and she dropped her arms around his neck.

The change made him pull from inside her. He took her arms a second time in his hands and drew them up over her head against the wood. "Stay there," he said, rather hissed at her, his look intent. Her eyes went wide but didn't blink when he invaded her a second time. His mouth found her neck, sucked deeply and he didn't care a purple mark would appear later. Corin started to shift over his hand and he slipped a second finger inside her while he latched onto her nipple.

Corin took what he offered and wanted more, slowly moving over him in small circles, forcing his fingers to move with her instead of her against him. She closed her eyes and took everything he gave.

He dropped to his knees before her and stroked her with his tongue in a rhythm that matched her inner muscles. She groaned and dropped her arms beside her, but didn't reach to touch him, rather to balance herself. He'd explored her last night, but this was different, primal in the way his tongue and fingers worked her body. Corin reached down with one hand and held his head to her, his hair threading through her fingers.

He changed the pattern of his kiss and she groaned as her insides clutched then moistened his fingers. He stayed with her, slowing his movements until she opened her eyes. He stood before her and dragged his fingers across her lips, moistening them with her release. Corin let her tongue slip out to follow their path then sucked them deeper into her mouth.

Tom let out a growl and quickly turned her around, pushing her against the door while he tugged her jeans further down her thighs. He stood behind her, took her in one smooth motion until he was buried inside her. His fingers bit into her hips pulling her over him, setting the pace. She was using her hands to balance against the door but dropped one to where they were joined, stroking the junction lightly, feeling each thrust.

Tom took her neck under his lips, just short of biting her when he finally relented and let himself take his own freedom. His breathing began to normalize and he realized he'd taken her against the door this time. He was shaking his head as he disentangled from her, accepting her weight against his chest so she wouldn't collapse. His arm dropped under her butt and lifted her into his arms, taking the few steps needed to reach the bed. He laid her carefully on the edge and followed down beside her, his lips to her for long minutes.

"Damn it, Corin, you've got me taking you like an animal against the door. First the counter last night, now this." His large fingers stroked along her chest and rib cage.

"Tommy, do it again," was all she told him as she took his hand and slipped it down her body, the pressure of her fingers pushing his inside her. He followed her command and watched as she moved over him, used him as a tool to find her completion. When it struck, her whole body quaked under him.

Corin groaned in the same movement and her hands drew him to her face, her lips taking his in an act of want and need. When he pulled away she wasn't happy, her eyes snapping open to watch him.

"Stay there, Corin," he managed to tell her before moving to strip her pants the rest of the way down her legs. He dropped down and laved her swollen lips, savoring the taste of her release, now mixing with his own. When he moved back up her body he inserted himself in one smooth movement, her body taking him deeply as his lips shared their essence. She sighed under him and opened to him.

Neither of them slept, rather dozed on and off a few times. When the sun rose Corin was straddling Tom's legs, her head thrown back in abandon while she rode him to fulfillment. His hands steadied her hips and with each downward stroke he pushed up towards her. Tom knew she was nearing the imaginary edge but wasn't finding it, still searching for it. He let his left hand drop between their bodies, his fingers grazing them.

Corin felt the difference and leaned into him further, taking his offering and using him to find the split second when she'd let herself free fall. When it happened there were no screams or gasps. She simply let her body melt down over his, keeping his hand trapped between them, moving her hips to keep him from stopping.

Tom gave her a minute to catch her breath then turned her under him, taking her hand to the same junction. Her slim fingers wrapped around his shaft, another layer to thrust through forcing him to abandon his willpower and let the inevitable happen. His raspy voice let out a bellowing howl. His body glistened with a layer of sweat from his strenuous actions and Corin ran her hands down his chest and across his belly, leaving lines in the moisture.

"Morning," she said with an impish grin.

"Morning," he uttered before he moved beside

her and dropped his weight onto the mangled sheets. "Damn it, Corin, are you trying to give me a heart attack..."

As soon as the words left his lips he wished he could pull them back. He felt her stir beside him and closed his eyes against the inevitable. When he thought she would pull away from him she surprised him and moved closer to his body, fitting herself against him.

"Its okay, Tom, Rand was jogging when he died, thank God, or we'd really have another problem to deal with." She smiled at him and leaned up, propping her head on her hand. "There's always going to be talk around us about car accidents, cheating husbands and people who die from heart attacks. You can't insulate me from all of it. I need you to be close by, to hold my hand or to give me that special look that reminds me you're here for me and our life together is more important than the past we can't change."

"I love you, Corin. I will to the day I die." She dropped down and gave him a wet sloppy kiss on his cheek.

"I love you, too. And I didn't hyperventilate when you said the word, die."

"All right, I'll try to relax."

"Any way I can help..." she asked as her fingers drew down along his chest.

"Make it last night so we have more time together. Can you do that?"

"No. If I could I would, for us." He sighed resignedly.

"What happens now?"

"Well, that depends on your stamina!" She let her hands trace over him and found he did have on ticklish spot that she didn't refrain from stroking. When the tenseness seemed gone, she pulled back, suddenly serious.

"In a few hours I'll get on a plane for home and you'll continue on with the tour. And God willing, the next few months won't be as horrible as we're both assuming they're going to be."

"And after that?"

"I guess we'll just have to wait and see what happens. You may decide this isn't what you thought it would be, Tom. I came here prepared for that possibility. I'm very glad it wasn't a reality, but it might be in the future." His fingers tangled in her hair and drew her head down to his, stopping just a breath away from his mouth.

"Never, I love you in a way I've never loved before. If I didn't this wouldn't be so difficult. I'd be able to let you go and not regret it."

"No regrets, Tom. I came here because I wanted to be with you, the man. Not the friend or musician. Just you stripped bare, without any outside influences. I wanted to know how you'd make me feel, how you'd touch me."

"Am I on the right track?" His fingers loosened in her hair but neither of them moved.

"Beyond my wildest dreams, and believe me, Tommy, since you left me last September, I've been dreaming." She sealed her words with a kiss that took them to the beginning once again, this time slow and languid, knowing it was one last time. With each move or touch they told each other how much they cared and loved.

****

For Corin, the worst part was actually leaving him. They'd stayed in bed until the last possible moment, relenting only to shower and dress. Her car to the airport would arrive shortly and she knew he'd have to get on the road. She'd asked him not to come down with her and he understood why. Neither of them wanted any public displays. What they shared was private, for their memories only.

Standing in the small hallway, reluctant to leave, she turned back for one last hug.

"Thank you for coming to me," he said with his lips pressed against her temple.

"Thank you for making me come!" She pulled back and smiled adding, "Again and again and again..."

"All right smartass, enough," he said, finally smiling.

"You realize it would be different if we decide to make this permanent. Our lives will get caught up in the every day stuff that makes it life and our sex lives will be affected."

"As long as we're together, we make our own reality, one we're both comfortable with." They held on for long minutes, neither willing to let go. When the phone rang he reluctantly moved to answer it, telling the caller she'd be down shortly. She gave him a curt nod and squared her shoulders.

"I was so nervous about coming here, about your reactions, if I'd disappoint you? I never gave any thought to how I'd feel when it came time to leave."

"Then don't go. It's just that simple." She gave him a rueful smile. "All right, but it is an option."

"One I'll take you up on shortly."

"Promise?"

"Yes, soon."

"I love you Corin, don't ever question that under any circumstances."

"I love you too, Tom. And I'll come back when I'm whole and can offer myself to you completely." She leaned up and kissed him before turning and pulling open the door, stopping any further discussions or displays.

For Corin it was as if she'd known him all her life, his touch something she was missing only until now she hadn't known it was absent from her life. She'd known instantly this was meant to be. She had to know for herself if it was all in her mind or if Tom really did make her feel what she was experiencing. After this weekend, there was no doubt left. She was head over heels in love with Tom Hayden.

****

Tom sat on the edge of the bed, the plaid flannel shirt she had on the first night she came to him pressed against his face, her scent embedded in the fabric. He'd gone to throw his shaving kit in his bag and saw it neatly folded on top, a Godiva chocolate bar peaking from the pocket. He laughed, and then held back the threatening tears. He had to believe she'd come back to him. And he had to give her the distance to do it on her own terms, no matter how much it annoyed or distressed him.

Chapter Thirteen

Tom thought it odd Joe wanted to change the encore to Another Man's Love. They hadn't played it in public yet and he wasn't sure why tonight was different.

"I don't know, just figured we'd see what kind of reception it got. Let's just see how we feel later, no pressure." Joe had wandered away but left Tom with a strange feeling.

They were giving their last performance at Madison Square Garden in New York City before taking a well-deserved two-week break. After that, they'd head west for the last leg of the tour before getting some down time to work on the new album in the fall.

Tom thought Joe and Anna seemed flustered but didn't ask, he figured they were just antsy to get home. He'd already decided not to stay in the city, he made arrangements to have his driver rested and ready when the show ended to take him directly back to Boston. By morning, he'd be home, a place he grew more attached to each time he came back to it. He decided it was because that was where he'd hung Corin's portrait. In the past, his house was always just a house. A place to kick back and store everything he had but didn't appreciate.

After the first of the year he'd seen the structure differently and he knew it was because of Corin's influence. Would she be comfortable there, could she turn it into a real home for them both? The questions had been too numerous to deal with, so instead, he tried to see it as she might, through her eyes. He'd been deciding what changes to make and figured it would be best to let Corin see it before doing anything structural.

Of course, that meant she would have to actually get to Boston and since she'd only left one message with him since their meeting in Dallas, the idea wasn't promising.

He didn't restrain himself the first week in April. He'd gotten her machine and left only a quick, "It's Tom and you've been on my mind. I know this must be a difficult time for you, I hope you're all right."

She hadn't called back and they were already two weeks into May. He pushed the memory aside when his assistant breezed past and told him it was five minutes to stage time.

Once he set foot in front of the crowd, he let his mind go blank, only the music mattered for the next hour. Tom and Joe were half way through their performance when they slowed the tempo a bit, playing a few older songs from their first albums. Then he glanced towards the right. He glimpsed Anna with the twins standing in front of her. But beside her he saw Corin.

While he didn't forget the music, his mind went on autopilot. A second glance and he decided he'd been wrong. That couldn't bc Corin, that would mean she was in New York. It struck him the woman beside Anna was Corin, but she'd changed.

This woman, his woman was striking. She wore straight black leather pants with slim heeled boots. Her black suede jacket was layered over a soft looking white turtleneck sweater. Her hair was long, longer than when he'd first met her and definitely longer than when he'd seen her last February. Her make-up was flawless, her face radiant with a hint of mischief. Anna's smile was beaming too wide to be missed. Barely managing to get through the set, he all but bolted off the stage towards her. A stage hand tossed him a towel which he used to dry his face before moving towards her. Corin stood tall as he approached.

"Are you really here?" he asked, his right hand going to stroke her cheek.

"Only if you want me to be."

"I want, Corin. God, I want so much." He dropped his lips to hers in a light kiss without a thought of who was watching. The applause was rampant in the back ground and he knew he had to go back for the encore. "Wait here, don't disappear," he whispered before turning back towards the stage.

He and Joe moved back to their places in the spotlight, both with guitar in hand. Tom quieted the crowd before speaking.

"Tonight, we have a surprise. This is off the new album and you'll be the first to hear it, let us know what you think." He nodded to Joe and the lighting changed. The whole arena went black for several seconds before two spots opened up, one on each of the men.

"This is called, "Another Man's Love," he told the crowd before playing the first chords. The words and music flowed from him, emotions pent up for over a year forced their way into his performance. His voice was strong and clear as he sang:

"We were never supposed to meet, But fate called our bluff,

She's everything I ever wanted, But dared not dream,

She's another man's love, She doesn't notice me

She's another man's love, She'll never be free,

I have no choice, I walk away, Searching for another way,

Her face invades my dreams,

She never fades away,

She's another man's love, She doesn't notice me,

She's another man's love, She'll never be free,

Time finds us, but is it too late, No longer his wife, I can't walk away,

A second chance to make her mine, Dare I imagine,

No longer his wife, I make her mine,

She's my wife now, I'll never set her free."

When the last note sounded the lights went down and the crowd went crazy with applause. Tom didn't notice any of it, he moved from the stage and handed the instrument to a waiting hand and grabbed for Corin, dragging her backstage. Somehow the crew seemed to know he wanted privacy and normal routine was excused. He pulled her into a dressing room and blocked the door with his body.

"Are you really here, here to stay, Corin?"

"For as long as you want me."

His arms opened to her and she let him swallow her up against his body for the kiss he'd been dreaming about. Noise from the hallway ultimately interrupted them.

"Go, do what you have to, but, when you can get away...Tom, there's something I want to show you." He nodded before opening the door to let reality back into their lives, if only temporarily.

He went through the backstage motions; signed compact discs and stood for photos with fans. He'd grabbed Corin's hand as they hurried towards his waiting car. He stopped dead about ten feet from the black vehicle when he saw Beau's large head and sad eyes pop through the half open window beside the driver. He detoured to pet the beast and was dutifully rewarded with a half howl half bark. When they were safely encased in the back of the limousine he finally attempted to talk.

"How?" was all he managed before dragging her face towards his. It was a long time before she was able to answer and when she did it was with a smile.

"Anna managed to scrounge me up a back stage pass."

"How long, Corin?"

"For as long as you want me, us," she corrected, including Beau. "We're a package deal."

"I'm all for packages, Corin, especially yours." He glanced out the window and saw they were heading towards Greenwich Village. "What's going on?"

"Something I wanted to show you," she whispered before taking his mouth under hers. The vehicle stopped before she pulled away from Tom's lips and hands. She nodded for him to get out and he reluctantly opened the car door.

He glanced to the gallery before them, several large works in the front window. Corin stood beside him, quiet. He looked to her again and found she wasn't giving him any hints. Only then did he really look at the canvases. It struck him as if he'd been hit. A slow smile formed on her lips. Tom studied each picture, more amazed than he would have believed possible.

Before him were three pictures of coastlines. They were blurred black and white photographs that had been flushed in with water paint. While the colors were muted they gave a life to the photograph behind them. He saw how she'd layered shade and texture and realized he'd never seen anything quite like them.

"I've been busy," she started.

"They're amazing, Corin. What gave you the idea?"

His arm automatically went to her shoulder, pulling her to his body. It was a simple gesture she returned, wrapping her arm around his waist.

"Christmas, I was down in Florida and started taking photos to learn how to use the digital camera Dad bought me. When I got home it just fell into place. A friend showed me how to use the computer to enhance the image and another how to transfer it to canvas."

"Call the gallery owner and tell them they're sold," he said, not bothering to wait for her reaction.

"That's one possibility, but I figured another was to use the photos I take while on tour with you this summer for yours. They'll have more meaning if they are places we visited together."

"We can hang them in the living room, interspersed with the water colors I bought last year." He waited for her response and was rewarded with a blank stare. "You didn't think I'd let them go, did you?"

"I never thought about it...Once I ship them up here, I have to let go of the work."

"You do, I didn't." He gave her a faint smile and she started to laugh.

"I suppose we have a lot to learn about each other."

"We have the rest of our lives..."

"Are you going to keep every canvas I do?"

"Possibly..."

"We're going to need a lot of wall space!" He turned to stare, afraid he might have misunderstood. "If you haven't changed your mind, that is?" She held back a grin and he pulled her to him.

"Why now?"

"Because the time was right; I'd found myself and my work again. And I missed you terribly."

"Those are the nicest words you've ever said to me," he said with a smile.

"How about, I love you and want to be with you, for as long as you'll have me?"

"Those are even better."

"Tom, thank you for understanding and for giving me the time to heal."

"Anything for my wife," he said before they were

interrupted by Beau's howling bark for attention.

"Are you sure, about being your wife? Maybe we should just live together for a while and see how it goes?" He watched her intently before laughing.

"Feel better you got that out?" Tom leaned forward resting his forehead against hers, his hands angling her chin towards him. "Corin, are you going to drive me crazy about this? I've never wanted to marry a woman so badly in my life. I want everyone to know we're together and they aren't welcome in our world."

"After making you wait so long...Tommy, you're sure?"

"Absolutely, remember the lyrics to the song? It's what kept me going all these months. I had to believe you'd come to me, but I knew it had to be in your own time."

"Tommy, take me home,"

"To North Carolina?" he asked a mischievous grin on his lips.

"No, to Boston, take me home to Boston." She pulled back but let her fingers mingle in his blonde hair. "Tommy, I learned something very important since September," Corin started, then slipped her index finger against his lips when he might have spoken.

He watched her gather courage with a deep breath before continuing. "I learned that home isn't a structure for me anymore, home is where you are. So if it's Boston or on the road, I want us to be together."

"Anything you say, Mrs. Hayden..." He hurried her towards the waiting car and then paused to take a last look at her art work before closing them in the privacy of the car.

The drive to Boston went slowly, keeping hormones and emotions in check until they finally pulled up before a sprawling multi-level house high up on a bluff. They'd held each other tightly during the ride but were loathe to start anything physical. They needed privacy and to talk and Tom didn't want their first time together to be in the back seat of a car, even if it was a chauffeur driven one.

He'd closed his eyes for a few moments when Corin relaxed beside him, snuggling deeper towards him. She slept quietly against his chest, her hand resting over his heart. He'd fallen asleep too, rousing before Corin stirred, watching the rise and fall of her chest with each breath.

The wood structure in front of them was part post-and-beam, part log cabin. Large expanses of glass overlooked the ocean far below them. To the side was a glass-enclosed pool.

"Tommy, it's beautiful," Corin said as he opened the front door. She laughed when he grabbed her around the waist and tossed her over his shoulder before entering.

"It will be once you turn it into our home. I don't want a house anymore; I want us to have a home."

"So do I." He set her on her feet just inside the main living area. The vaulted ceiling was balanced by a three-story stone fireplace with the stonework chimney rising high through the roof, Tom moved easily towards it and bent down to set a match to the waiting kindling.

Standing, he watched Corin take in the room around them. He noticed his driver bringing in the last of their luggage along with a fifty pound bag of dog food, Beau's leash in one hand on his last trip to the door. After thanking the man and letting Beau free to roam his new space he leaned against one of the large posts to watch Corin.

She was taking in every detail of the room, from the planked ceilings to the tinted windows that made up the far wall. Her gaze fixed on the ocean, the waves crashing against the beach front.

****

Tom wanted to grab her and take her to bed. Instinct told him to go a bit slower especially after their time in Dallas. He left her to admire the boulders that anchored the hearth, her hand ran over the coarse texture. To her left was a large, open dining room, the mahogany table big enough to comfortably seat ten. Beyond that was the open kitchen. Corin wandered around the space and finally found him in the kitchen, the coffee pot pulled towards him.

"It's an amazing space, Tom. How long have you lived here?" She'd discarded her jacket along the way and now he could see her soft curves highlighted by the sweater. He nodded when she automatically moved towards a cabinet, assuming that was where the coffee mugs would be.

"I've owned it for five years but I've probably only spent a total of two actually living in it. I usually spent time in the islands after touring. I'd come back here when it was time to write the next album."

He measured out coffee grounds and switched on the pot before returning them to the freezer. Opening the refrigerator door he laughed. "I asked my housekeeper to get some basics in, but somehow I think she was tutored."

He pulled out a platter with cheese chunks and several varieties of grapes covered with plastic. Next came a bottle of white wine and bowl of deep red cherries. Corin had wandered around the room and studied it quickly.

"I was debating about doing some updating these last months, but wanted to see what you thought." Tom Hayden was blunt if nothing else. Somehow it eased the nerves tightening in his stomach.

"That's what you were thinking?" The long work

counter in the center of the room separated them. "What else have you been thinking, Tom?"

"All sorts of wonderful things, Corin, like how I'd finally get the chance to undress you before that warm fire in there." He opened the bottle of wine and slowly poured the liquid into two cobalt blue wine glasses. With his back to her as he replaced the wine in the fridge, he continued. "I wondered what it would feel like to wake up in the middle of the night and find you cuddled against me, or how you'd look as I made love to you in the early morning. Dallas was a tease, Corin. A quick glimpse of heaven and then you were gone. I don't want that to happen ever again."

Heat flashed through Corin's body with each suggestive word he uttered. "What else?" she prompted as he approached her, holding out one of the glasses for her.

"I've thought about selling this place and finding something you'd like better. This isn't anything like your home. I decided I'd show you around the area and let you pick a place you'd be comfortable."

"Are you comfortable here, Tom? Does this place have memories for you?" It was a valid question and he understood her motives in asking, especially after his understanding about her home with Rand.

"I've lived here alone since I moved in, Corin. No girlfriend or wife has spent time here."

"I definitely want to explore the town and learn my way around." She drifted towards the fire, dropping before it, her glass safely put to the side. Tom carried the plates to the coffee table before the fireplace, shaking his head at Beau stretched out in peaceful slumber on his leather couch. He bought some time by stacking several large logs on the burning embers before dropping down on a large leather club chair across from her. Staring at the flames Corin finally found her voice.

185

"Thank you for telling me no other woman has been here. It shouldn't matter but it does." She glanced to him but averted her eyes quickly when she realized he was studying her.

"This is my space, Corin and now I'm offering to share it with you."

"We need to clarify a few things all right?" Corin sat tall and drew a breath. "I finally finished getting Rand's estate straightened out. I've set up a scholarship fund with the proceeds from his last book. It will come out next fall. The publisher will oversee it." She reached for her glass but only moistened her lips with the liquid. "I'll always love him, Tom. I couldn't have married him if I didn't. But I've had to put him and our marriage in perspective. And I've had to let him go."

Tom tipped his glass towards the meaning behind her words but didn't offer any of his own. "And I've come to realize it's not necessarily the structure itself, it's the person you're with that makes a house a home."

"What about the house at Wrightsville?"

"It's a home I used to live in with my second husband. He's gone and so is the feeling of the place. Now it's just a house. I can let it go, as long as I have a home with you."

"Always, Corin, no matter where we are, just you and me."

"And Beau?" she questioned with a laugh, spotting the old hound sprawled out on the living room sofa.

"And Beau too."

****

Corin looked around the room, the sunrise just hinted at morning, lighting up the space. "I like this house Tom. It has a good feel to it, like it was just waiting to be loved." She stood slowly before heading to the kitchen, returning with two steaming mugs in her hand.

"I have a studio downstairs, Corin. There's another room that might work as your studio or the third floor might have better light, your call. Any or all of it can be modified."

"I'll explore them later. Tommy, come here," she whispered as her hand extended towards him. For several seconds he didn't react and when he did it wasn't the reaction Corin expected.

"Hold that thought, I'll be right back." He put his mug aside and disappeared up the open staircase and into the far door, returning shortly with a slight smile on his lips.

Tom moved through the room calmly while watching her intently. He dropped his body on the edge of the coffee table and seemed to be steadying himself.

"Corin, you know I fell in love with you at first sight and there was nothing I could do about it. Now I can." She watched him closely wondering what he'd say next. "I'm asking you to marry me, Corin Toscano Shephard, to be my wife, for the rest of our lives."

"Yes," was all she managed to get out before rising towards him. Tom let his arms take her against him, finally having her close. The kiss they shared was different from any other time they'd been close. She'd surrendered to him and they both knew the difference. Tom pulled back only slightly before reaching for her hand. He slid a gold band onto her left third finger then pulled her close again.

"Just give us some time, Corin, I know we can make this work. We have to; life isn't worth anything to me unless I have you beside me."

"Yes," was all she again managed. When she got the first look at the ring he'd placed on her finger she smiled boldly. A gold band with three matched one-carat diamonds anchored it. On either side was a small row of emeralds all fused into one band.

"For our pasts," he started, "For our present and especially for our future, Corin. I promise to try to make you happy every day for the rest of my life."

"I want that too, Tom. I want to be everything you deserve and more. I love the ring, thank you." She leaned forward and sealed their words with a kiss. "But more importantly, I love you, Tom. The man, not the performer, although I understand they're one and the same. I look at you, Tommy and get a static inside me that I've never known before, it just feels right for us." Corin's hands tugged his shirt from his jeans, her warm fingers slipping against his skin.

"Tommy..." she uttered, before getting lost in his kiss. They managed to make it to the bedroom hours later but sleep still wasn't on either of their minds. They'd consummated their love before the fireplace with the sun rising in the distance.

"Corin, welcome home," he'd whispered just before filling her for the first time in their bed.

Her reply had been a breathless, "Yes."

****

They were married a week later, standing before the stone fireplace in the living room of the home they would now share. Joe and Anna were there with the girls as well as their tour manager, Greg. Corin's father had flown up with his new lady friend and Bob managed to make the last shuttle. At seven in the evening, Corin slowly descended the staircase towards her father waiting at the bottom. She wore a silver colored dinner suit that had a hint of green in the weave; her hair was long and loose. She carried a small nosegay of platinum roses. Tom waited for her, a black suit with a grey shirt making his features call to her. Their vows were said with clear minds and strong voices, the melody of their song playing low in the background. The judge who married them stayed long enough to share a glass of champagne before discreetly disappearing.

Their catered supper was served in the candle lit dining room and by ten everyone had been driven home or back to their hotel for the night. They would all regroup tomorrow afternoon for a late brunch before returning to their respective homes. Until then, they had the house to themselves and managed to tune out the rest of the world.

****

Tom lay naked across the king size bed in the master bedroom when Corin came from the bath. She was wearing a pale green gown of silk that pooled about her ankles, the lace covering her breasts almost translucent. Reaching a hand to her she slid easily against him.

"Thank you for making me your wife, Mr. Hayden," Corin said as her fingers ran through his hair, dragging his mouth towards hers.

"Anything to accommodate, Mrs. Hayden," he replied.

Hours later when they were sated and hungry again for food they found themselves in the kitchen, Corin wearing the dress shirt Tom had worn to marry her in. He was naked from the waist up, only a pair of worn jeans pulled up over his bottom half. They raided the leftovers from their wedding supper and while he was attempting to feed her a small bit of cake he paused, a strange look overtaking his face.

"What?" Corin asked.

"This may not be the right time, but I want you to think about something."

"All right, as long as it's not a divorce," she teased, suddenly anxious.

He seemed to read her emotions and pulled her close against his chest, his fingers tangling in her long curls.

"Don't panic. I just wanted you to know I've done

some checking and if you decide you want to, we can have my vasectomy reversed."

"You've done some checking," she teased. "I think that's a decision we'll leave until after the honeymoon." She rose up on her toes and dropped a light kiss on his lips. "I thought you didn't want children?"

"I said I didn't want my children to have *Amber* as their mother, you, my dear wife, are another story altogether."

"What if you reverse it and I can't conceive or carry to term?"

"We'll worry about that when it happens, if it happens. Besides, I figure the Powers That Be," he looked upward for a moment, "Well, I figure they have a master plan for us and we'll just have to go along with it. There's always adoption."

"You wouldn't mind?"

"We'll accept any children we're lucky enough to have, no matter who gives birth to them."

"I like that idea too. Thank you Tommy, for understanding me so well."

"I'm only going to ask one thing from you and its non negotiable." She nodded and he continued. "Bob is never to bring any unattached straight men to our home, understand?" She laughed, her eyes filling but no tears fell.

"Actually, he and I had this discussion just last week!"

"God, I love you and the way your mind works."

"I love you too, Tom. For the last time in my life I'm in love. You do understand don't you?" Corin's hand slipped down and captured his growing awareness with her palm. She pumped him lightly several times and watched his eyes slowly close.

"You're the woman I always dreamed of and never knew existed."

"Until the third week in February..."

"You realize I can never sell that blasted truck now?"

"We'll park it on the lawn and turn it into a fountain and planter..."

"It's one option, only first I get to make love to my wife in the back seat..."

"Only once," she asked, before adding, "Whatever you say...wherever you say."

Epilogue

Five years later

Corin stood in the dining room of their home surveying the table setting. Tonight she and Tom would celebrate their fifth wedding anniversary. They had come a long way together in these first years, she thought with a smile.

After the first six months on tour they decided they could weather anything together since they'd managed to orient themselves on the road. Humor and love saw them through the unexpected problems and interruptions.

Photography had become her new profession, her photos showing a new depth in her life. She liked the anonymity of having a different type of canvas to work with. They'd done some minor renovations to their home, the third floor becoming her light infused studio.

Tom had his vasectomy reversed and they decided to try and adopt, taking off the pressure she might feel if unsuccessful at conceiving. That pressure was relieved when they were accepted as adoptive parents three years ago. Their daughter came to them at age two, already named Jun, which meant truth in Chinese. They added Ella to her name which meant born in June, the month she came into their lives. Junella was healthy and happy, and their hearts desire. They were all learning to speak Ella's heritage language to keep a part of that alive for her. She'd taken to the piano without prompting and she and Tom were often surprised by her talent.

Corin never doubted Tom's ability as a parent, his love encompassed them all as a warm blanket of security, trust and love.

Tonight, her dad would bring his new wife to the celebration, having decided they wanted to be married as opposed to keeping pensions and benefits. He seemed happy, that was all that mattered.

Bob was in residence for the weekend, along with his new partner, Trevor, an antique dealer she introduced him to a few years back. They seemed an immediate fit, but she refrained from pushing. On their own they were finding their new life together.

She and Anna had become fast friends, bonding on the road over family and business. Their twins were in their last year of high school and already looking into colleges.

In a few weeks they would head back on tour for six months with Hayden and Haas' new album, *Same People-New Beginnings*. While their style had changed, their music matured, opening doors to new listeners.

Ella had already made her first music tour and was looking forward to the bus ride. This would be the first time Jack Henry would travel with them. At fourteen months old, she doubted he'd remember it, but she'd have photos to remind him. At first she couldn't believe she'd really conceived and it was Tom's constant smile that made the pregnancy a breeze. Jack's delivery was another story, but they'd all made it through.

She glanced over her shoulder towards the indoor pool hearing the children's laughter, Tom and Bob each had a child safely in hand, teaching them the finer arts of swimming.

When the party ended tonight, she'd give Tom his special present. Just past her second month, she felt good and the doctors assured her that they, she and the baby, were both healthy. If things worked out, they'd just be finishing the tour when this one was ready to make its appearance.

She'd sold the North Carolina house with no regrets, her home now with Tom, whether in Boston or their tour bus. When she thought back to her life before Tom, it all seemed like a misty dream. She'd always have Rand safely tucked in her heart, but Tom and her family were her reality, one she cherished every day.

About the author...

Having been born and raised on Long Island, NY, my husband and I were both eager to leave the urban lifestyle behind us and explore our futures.

With his encouragement I'm living my dream of writing romance novels full time. Our new rural setting allows us time to enjoy each other and leaves me guiltless hours in my imagination indulging my other passion.

Visit Cheryl at www.cornellromance.com

Thank you for purchasing
this Wild Rose Press publication.
For other wonderful stories of romance,
please visit our on-line bookstore at
www.thewildrosepress.com.

For questions or more information,
contact us at info@thewildrosepress.com.

The Wild Rose Press
www.TheWildRosePress.com